"There Are Only Seven Probes . . ."

Lieutenant Dax pointed out. "That means two of us will have to stay behind."

On the bridge of the dying *Starship Defiant,* Captain Benjamin Sisko shook his head. "One more besides me," he said calmly.

"Benjamin," Dax began, "I—"

"I'm invoking the Captain's Privilege," Sisko stated firmly, "to go down with his ship."

"But sir—" Chief O'Brien objected.

"I'm not inviting any further discussion," Captain Sisko said. "Case closed."

Look for STAR TREK Fiction from Pocket Books

Star Trek: The Original Series

Star Trek: The Next Generation

Star Trek: Deep Space Nine

Star Trek: Voyager

STAR TREK
DEEP SPACE NINE®

SARATOGA

Michael Jan Friedman

POCKET BOOKS

New York   London   Toronto   Sydney   Tokyo   Singapore

This book is a work of fiction. Names, characters, places and incidents are products of the author's imagination or are used fictitiously. Any resemblance to actual events or locales or persons, living or dead, is entirely coincidental.

An *Original* Publication of POCKET BOOKS

POCKET BOOKS, a division of Simon & Schuster Inc.
1230 Avenue of the Americas, New York, NY 10020

A VIACOM COMPANY

STAR TREK is a Registered Trademark of Paramount Pictures.

This book is published by Pocket Books, a division of Simon & Schuster Inc., under exclusive license from Paramount Pictures.

ISBN: 0-671-56897-3

First Pocket Books printing November 1996

10 9 8 7 6 5 4 3 2 1

POCKET and colophon are registered trademarks of Simon & Schuster Inc.

Printed in the U.S.A.

For Harvey Ehrlich, wonder and inspiration

I'll make it short and sweet this time. After all, I'm really happy with the way this journey turned out, and I wouldn't want you to wait any longer than necessary to embark on it.

First, I'd like to thank John Ordover, world's fastest and friendliest editor, for buying this book in the first place and then being such a good and responsible partner throughout the creative process. John is a remarkable mixture of talent and humility—one of those guys who has a lot to crow about, yet never feels the need.

Second, I'd like to thank my wife and sons for their usual tolerance. Even the little one's starting to figure out what a deadline means.

Finally, I'd like to thank comic dealer Bob Jones of the Baltimore area—who had absolutely nothing to do with this book. On the other hand, he gave me tickets to an Orioles game once, just out of the goodness of his heart, and I never got around to thanking him for it. If you're out there, Bob, I enjoyed the game.

HISTORIAN'S NOTE

The events in *Saratoga* occur between the third and fourth seasons of *Star Trek: Deep Space Nine*.

Prologue

OLD FRIENDS, THOUGHT Pernon Obahr. You come to know them as you know yourself, to love them, to rely on them. You allow yourself to believe they will never let you down.

And yet, in the course of time, even the oldest friend may betray you. It was a fact of life, he mused—not only on Bajor, but on any world in the great, star-spanning cosmos.

Pernon stood on the highest balcony of the highest building in Karvis and followed the curve of the glistening river with his gaze. On its near bank, a few kilometers north of the city, a half-dozen large gray water pumps worked with the power and perserverance of prehistoric animals.

It was a good thing, too. Thanks to the pumps, some thirty percent of the river's volume was redirected through a channel that bisected the city. At the other end of the channel, the river water fanned out along a steep incline, eventually spilling into the sea.

Were the pumps not there, the city would have been washed away long ago. If that had happened, Pernon and his family would have been left penniless, destitute, like a great many other Bajorans at the time. Hence, his abiding love for the machines, a love shared in full by his fellow Karvisians.

But circumstances change, he thought. *All manner of things decay. And what a man thought was solid as a rock in his youth turns out to have been anchored in shifting sands.*

The words were those of Inartha Dor, one of Bajor's greatest poets before the Occupation. But they fit the situation, Pernon told himself—fit it as a hand fits a well-made glove.

After three decades, the pumps were beginning to fail—not because they were structurally unsound, for they had been given a good deal of attention over the years. No, the machines themselves were not the problem.

It was the power source that made them run. *That* was the problem. And if it were not solved, Karvis would eventually be destroyed.

Pernon sighed. As a youth, he had seen the birth of the pumps. He had witnessed the arrival of the Cardassian architects and the terrain engineers, the excavation specialists and the builders. He had watched the ground vehicles converge on the river-bank day after day, bringing all kinds of construction devices and raw materials.

Of course, for the Cardassians, the pumping station was a bandage on a self-inflicted wound. To obtain cheap power farther north, they had meddled with the river's tributaries. The result had been a massive increase in volume and several bad floods the following spring.

This was not pleasing to the Gul responsible for the area—a scaly-necked festival pole of a man named Divok. After all, it was Divok's head that would roll if the problem were not corrected somehow.

The point of the occupation had been to exploit Bajor's resources with a minimum of effort. Wiping out a fair-sized city was not part of the plan, nor did the Cardassian authorities wish to deal with additional backlash.

There was already a resistance movement brewing. Why fuel it any more than they had to?

Even as a boy, Pernon had hated the Cardassians as much as any Bajoran. He had detested them with every drop of blood in his body, with every muscle and every bone. Had he seen the pumps as something Cardassian, he would certainly have hated them as well.

But right from the start, he saw the lack of enthusiasm in the building of the things. The invaders had fitted the pieces together methodically, as if they themselves were nothing more than automatons. There was no joy in the project for them.

And even when they were finished, the Cardassians seemed only to tolerate the machines as a necessary evil. That, as much as anything else, made Pernon see the pumps as something Bajoran.

"Obahr? Is that you?"

Pernon turned at the sound of the familiar female voice. As he watched, his friend emerged from the shadows of the room behind him.

"Nerys," he said, glad for the opportunity to speak her name. "What's it been? Almost a year?"

"More like a year and a half," she told him, approaching with her arms thrown wide.

"You're kidding," he declared.

"I'd never try to kid an old resistance fighter," she assured him.

As they embraced, he remembered a time when he had hoped she would be more than a comrade. As it happened, the opportunity to express that hope had never materialized. And with their lives constantly on the line, he came to value her friendship too much to try to change it.

Kira leaned back to look at him. "You're gaining weight," she observed. "Being a city administrator agrees with you, I see."

"That's not it," he explained candidly. "I'm making up for all the times we went hungry fighting the Cardassians."

Her smile faded. "I remember." Then she patted him affectionately on the shoulder. "So what can I do for you, Pernon Obahr? Or were you serious when you asked me down here for a game of nob-noch?"

"Don't I wish," he replied.

That's when he told her about the pumps. And he told her some other things as well, things he had learned through the network of former resistance fighters—a network made more useful since Shakaar had come to power.

While Pernon spoke, Kira nodded. And when he was done, she nodded some more. Despite the circumstances, he couldn't help but remark inwardly on her beauty. It wasn't easy to pull his thoughts back on course.

"Do you think you can help?" he asked at last.

She looked at him. "I can try," she promised.

Pernon smiled with relief. When Kira Nerys said she would try, the reward was as good as won. It was good to know at least one old friend could still be counted on.

CHAPTER
1

JAKE SISKO LEANED over the rail of the Promenade's upper level and peered into Quark's. By craning his neck a little, he could see his father sitting at a table with Lieutenant Dax.

The elder Sisko was staring into his raktajino, an iced-coffee type drink. Even from here, Jake could see the crease in his father's brow.

"Jake?"

The boy turned to his companion, whose face barely cleared the rail. But then, Ferengi were among the smaller races that populated the station, and Nog—being a mere teenager—was shorter than most.

"Mm?" Jake replied.

"Why does your father look so depressed?" asked Nog.

The human sighed. "He's going to see some of his old cronies again."

The Ferengi looked at him. "And he's depressed about that?" He grunted. "They must not have been very good friends."

Jake scrutinized his father. "Actually, they were some of the best friends he's ever had. They served with him on his last assignment, the *Saratoga*. A couple of times, they even saved his life."

Nog shook his head. "Then why isn't he glad to see them?"

The human shrugged. "It's difficult to explain. You see, he'd have been happy to see any one of them, if he met them at another starbase or something. But this is an official occasion."

The Ferengi seemed to ponder the information. "Ah, an official occasion. I understand," he said with assurance. "Of course I understand. I mean, who *wouldn't* understand?"

He paused. "Jake?"

The boy glanced at him. "I know. You haven't the slightest idea of what I'm talking about."

"That's right," the Ferengi complained, unable to hide his exasperation. "What difference does it make if it's official or not? Friends are friends, aren't they?"

Jake shook his head. "Believe me," he said, "it makes a difference. Dad will be using the *Defiant* to take his old shipmates to the Utopia Planitia shipyards in orbit around Mars. That's where they'll witness the commissioning of the *new Saratoga*."

"The new *Saratoga?*" Nog echoed. He looked perplexed. "What happened to the *old Saratoga?*"

The boy was suddenly beset by memories, which not so long ago would have overwhelmed him. But he was older now. He could take a deep breath and wish them away.

"The old one," he said, in slow, careful tones, "was the ship where my mom was killed. You know, by the Borg."

He wasn't looking at his friend, but he could imagine the embarrassment on the Ferengi's face.

"Oh," declared Nog, in an artificially cheerful tone. "Now I remember." He paused. "So that's why it's so hard for your father to see these people together? Because they remind him of your mother's death?"

Jake nodded. "That's why," he answered.

It wasn't going to be easy for him, either. But more than himself, he was worried about his dad. As commanding officer of *Deep Space Nine,* the man seldom let on that he had feelings about anything.

But Benjamin Sisko's feelings ran deep indeed. And when it came to that terrible moment on the *Saratoga,* they ran so deep Jake had never seen the bottom of them.

Sisko turned to Dax. At some point, he had allowed their conversation to slip away from him.

"Did you say something?" he asked her.

The Trill regarded him with a mixture of compassion and rebuke. "I said a lot of somethings, Benjamin. At what point did you stop listening?"

The captain peered into his raktajino and frowned. "I'm sorry, Old Man. I just can't seem to concentrate on anything lately."

"Because all you can think about is the *Saratoga*," said Dax. "And seeing your fellow officers again."

He looked up at her. "You know, I'd come to grips with Jennifer's death. As far as I could tell, I'd accepted it. I'd put it behind me."

"Until you got that message from Starfleet," his friend suggested, "ordering you to ferry a bunch of *Saratoga* survivors to Mars."

Sisko sighed. "The wounds have closed," he explained, "but that doesn't mean they won't open again under the right circumstances."

"So I take it you're not looking forward to the ceremony at Utopia Planitia," Dax concluded.

He looked at her. "Not looking forward to it? I'd rather be dipped in Klingon hot sauce."

His companion shrugged. "Actually, I'm quite partial to Klingon hot sauce. Being dipped in it doesn't sound half-bad."

The captain frowned. "You know what I mean."

In her several previous lives as a joined Trill, Dax had been ambassador and artist, male and female, scientist and explorer. All that life experience had endowed her not only with a playful sense of humor, but with a keen and penetrating intelligence.

"If that's the case," she remarked sympathetically, "maybe you'd better not go to Utopia Planitia."

The captain straightened. "Not attend, you mean?"

She nodded. "You know, decline the invitation—as

respectfully as possible, of course. Tell them things are just too grim here at the station, what with the Dominion knocking at the door and Bajor on the perpetual brink of disaster." She grunted. "Actually, it won't be that far from the truth."

He shook his head. "But I *can't* decline."

"Why not?" asked the Trill.

Sisko held out his hands in an appeal for reason. "I'm the old *Saratoga*'s highest-ranking survivor. I've *got* to go. I owe it to all those people who died—not to mention those who *lived.*"

"That's a lousy reason," she pointed out.

The captain disagreed. He was about to say so when his companion forged on, her blue eyes suddenly alive with purpose.

"Don't do it for all those others," she told him, jabbing a forefinger in his direction. "Do it for *yourself,* Benjamin."

Sisko eyed her. "For myself?" he echoed.

"That's right," said Dax, smiling. "Because you're alive. Because you gave everything you had to that proud old ship. And most of all, because deep down inside, you really *want* to." She leaned forward. "Maybe it'll be a little uncomfortable for you, at first. I don't doubt that. But in the end, you'll have a good time. I know you will."

The captain couldn't help but smile back, albeit with a certain wariness. That's how infectious his friend's enthusiasm was.

He eased back in his seat. "You know me that well, do you?"

Dax grunted. "Who knows you better?"

Sisko regarded her for a moment, drawing confidence from her. Finally, he accepted the situation. "Done," he told her. "I just hope you're right about this, Old Man."

Her smile turned impish. "Benjamin," she said, "when have I ever steered you wrong?"

Quark smiled. Everyone in the place seemed to be enjoying himself—or herself, as the case might be. Even Captain Sisko, who'd seemed down in the dumps until just a few moments ago.

The Ferengi liked seeing people happy. When they were happy, they ate and drank more. They spent more money. And that made Quark happy.

To top off his delight, the long-necked, scaly-skinned Lu'ufan at the other end of the bar was describing to yet another innocent bystander the size of the *merragat* worm he'd snared for his sister's wedding feast.

Bending down, the Ferengi reached under his bar for the naturally cultivated *erriz* pod that he kept there. He'd only recently acquired a couple gross of the pods, which were perfect for cleaning delicate surfaces. Also, he'd gotten a great deal on them. And as the Rules of Acquisition clearly stated: *When you see a good deal, jump on it.*

Of course, at this rate, Quark would go through his whole supply of *erriz* pods before the week was out. But he didn't mind.

The reason for his tolerance manifested itself a

moment later—as the Lu'ufan made a particularly expansive gesture and knocked over his drink. The slushy yellow and brown contents of his Scintaavian Sunset spilled out over the previously spotless surface of the bar.

Whirling, the Lu'ufan gasped at his clumsiness. But before he could exhale, the Ferengi was on top of things. With a few circular swipes of his *erriz* pod, he sopped up the mess. Then, with a flourish, he righted the Lu'ufan's tall, fluted glass.

"Oh, my," he said, picking up the vessel, which was now empty except for a viscous yellow sediment along its insides. "It seems you've spilled your drink. *Again.*"

The Lu'ufan sighed—a response which included a pronounced, almost comical rise and fall of his very angular shoulders. "It seems I have," he agreed. "Spilled it, that is. Again."

"And you'd like another?" Quark ventured.

"Yes," said the Lu'ufan, "I would."

The Ferengi wagged a finger at him. "Try to take better care of this one, would you? The ingredients—"

"I know," the Lu'ufan interrupted. "They come from the planet Scintaavi—which no longer exists, since it was destroyed by a rogue comet several years ago."

"Along with the rest of its star system," Quark reminded him. "It's nothing less than sacrilege to waste such rare and exotic constituents."

The Lu'ufan nodded soberly. "And worse than that,

it is expensive." Taking another gold coin from his pocket, he laid it down on the bar. "Please. I'll be more careful this time. I promise."

"Well," said the Ferengi, in his most compassionate tone, "all right, then. I trust you." And with another swipe of the *erriz* pod for good measure, he went to mix his guest another drink.

Erriz pods didn't grow on trees, it was true. But considering what he was charging for his Scintaavian Sunsets, he might soon be able to buy his own pod farm.

"Brother?" called a familiar voice.

Quark turned and saw his sibling Rom advancing on the bar. He was carrying something wrapped in what looked like a bunch of rags. And he was smiling—always a bad sign when it came to Rom.

"What is it now?" asked Quark.

"Look what I found in the storeroom," said his brother. He held out the thing in his hands. "It was behind a case of *adjittari* wine. You know, the stuff we claim is ten years older than it really—"

Quark clamped his hand over his brother's mouth and looked around. Fortunately, no one seemed to have overheard Rom's indiscretion.

"Listen," rasped Quark. "I don't care where you found it. I don't even particularly care what it is. I just want to know if you've found out what I asked you to find out."

Rom regarded him with a certain amount of befuddlement. "And what was that, Brother?"

Quark cursed beneath his breath. How could he

and Rom have sprung from the same set of parents? It defied belief.

"I asked you to find out when the *Saratoga* survivors were going to arrive. You know, so we could hold some kind of event to honor them—an event that would draw people into the bar. You do remember that, don't you?"

His brother thought for a moment. Then, as he recalled Quark's instructions, he slapped his forehead with the heel of his hand.

"You're right, Brother. And I was going to find that out for you, I swear I was—until I realized we were out of those little *menju* nuts Morn is so fond of."

Quark grunted. "Morn's tab is longer than he is tall. You're forbidden to bring him any more nuts until he pays his bar bill."

Rom shook his head sheepishly. "All right, Brother. I won't bring him any more *menju* nuts. But the point I was making is that I had to go to the storeroom to get them. And while I was rummaging around for a fresh canister—"

He held up the thing in his hand. What's more, he seemed proud of it.

"—I discovered *this.*"

Quark sighed. "And what, pray tell, is that thing, anyway?"

Rom shrugged. "I don't know," he admitted. "I was kind of hoping you would be able to tell me."

With that, Rom began to peel away the rags. They didn't come away easily, and when they did they tended to fall apart. But eventually, he revealed enough of their contents for Quark to get an idea of what they were dealing with.

And when he did, it took his breath away.

The object was smoky blue and perfectly round, except for a small hole in the top of it. For the most part it looked smooth as glass, but there was a band of coarser material running around its circumference.

"By the Nagus," Quark breathed, reaching out for the thing involuntarily. "Do you know what that is?"

Rom rolled his eyes. "If I knew what it was, I wouldn't have asked you, Brother."

"It's a beverage container," Quark told him.

Rom tilted his head. "A beverage container?"

He took a step away from Quark, to view the object in a better light. But as he moved, his foot snagged on the base of one of the bar stools—and he stumbled, sending the smoky blue beverage container tumbling through the air.

Quark couldn't let the thing break—not when it was worth several times its weight in gold-pressed latinum. Diving full length, he reached out for the object in an attempt to catch it before it hit the ground.

He could feel his fingers grazing the beverage container, closing about it, trying to cradle it . . .

Then he hit the floor—hit it so hard, in fact, that his teeth rattled with the impact and the breath was knocked out of him.

"Brother, are you all right?"

As he lay on the floor, gasping for breath and

certain he'd broken some ribs, Quark found the strength to look up at Rom. Fortunately for his brother, Quark was in no position to throttle him, or he might have found himself an only child.

"Let me help you," Rom pleaded, grabbing Quark under his arms and pulling him up—whether Quark liked it or not.

It was the worried tone of Rom's voice that ultimately saved him from becoming a victim of fratricide. After all, how could Quark kill the only being in the universe who genuinely gave a spacer's damn about him?

"Leave me alone," he grated, still trying to catch his breath. "I'm fine, no thanks to you."

Slumping against the bar, he looked around and saw that several of his customers were staring at him. He smiled and waved a bit, to signify that he wasn't going to die and thereby release them from their obligations to him.

Besides, it didn't matter what kind of embarrassment he'd brought on himself—or to be more accurate, Rom had brought on him. The important thing, he reflected, as he looked down at his hands, was that he'd rescued the beverage container.

Setting the artifact down gently on the surface of the bar, Quark regarded it with an appropriate reverence. A moment later, he realized that his brother was gazing at it over his shoulder.

"I still don't understand," Rom told him. "If it's only a beverage container—"

"It's not just *any* beverage container," Quark informed him. He was almost able to speak normally now. "It's from Thetalian Prime."

His brother shook his head. "Thetalian Prime?"

"That's right," said Quark. "Thetalian Prime."

He lowered his voice, not wanting to tempt any thieves who might be in earshot. After all, one never knew.

"And like everything else made from the clay of that world," he went on, "it contains traces of corlandium. In case you haven't heard, that's a mineral. A rare and very valuable mineral."

Rom's eyes narrowed. "I *have* heard of it. And it's in that beverage container?" He leaned closer. "Are you sure?"

"Sure as I can be," Quark responded. "Of course, this thing would be even more valuable if the organisms that secreted the mineral were still alive. But then, it's not a perfect galaxy, is it?"

"Are you going to share the profits with me?" asked his brother.

"Most certainly not," Quark snapped. "By your own admission, you found this in my storeroom. And though I can't say exactly what container it fell out of, it clearly belongs to me."

Rom frowned. "Then you're right. It's *not* a perfect galaxy."

"I'd better lock this away," said Quark, pulling the beverage container to his bosom. "For safekeeping."

But he'd no sooner turned away from the bar than he found himself staring at a Bajoran uniform. And even before he looked up to see whose face went with it, he could tell from the way it was filled out whom it belonged to.

"Major Kira," he chuckled—a bit nervously, he thought. "To what do I owe the honor of this visit?"

Kira smiled. It was obvious from Quark's expression that he was trying to figure out what he'd done wrong.

But for a change, he hadn't done anything. Or at least, it wasn't any of the things he'd probably done that had brought her here.

"Please," she said. "The honor is all mine."

"It is?" Quark replied, clearly surprised.

"Of course," the Bajoran assured him. "I feel at home here. But then, maybe that's because I feel so at home with *you.*"

The Ferengi's smile faded. "You want something from me," he realized.

"Want something?" she repeated, as innocent as the day she was born.

"Come on," he told her. "Admit it."

"What makes you say I want something?" Kira inquired.

Quark frowned. "You can't con a con man, Major. You've been coming into my bar for years, and in all that time you've never said anything even vaguely nice to me. All of a sudden, you're treating me with respect—even affection. And you're telling me you don't *want* something?" He chuckled some more, this time honestly amused. "So what is it?"

The Bajoran sighed. "All right," she conceded. "Maybe I do have a bit of an ulterior motive."

"Aha," said the Ferengi, poking a finger at her. "I knew it."

"But what I'm asking isn't for me," she amended quickly. "It's for a place called Karvis. You may have heard of it."

Quark thought for a moment. "Karvis," he echoed. "Southern continent, yes? A medium-size city? At the mouth of the Teejan River, I believe?"

"That's the one," she told him. "Unfortunately, Karvis began flooding about thirty years ago—about the same time the Cardassians began tampering with the Teejan's tributaries. In order to preserve Karvis, they had to install a series of heavy-duty water pumps."

The Ferengi nodded. "Fascinating stuff," he said sarcastically. "But what's it got to do with me?"

"I'm getting to that," Kira assured him. "You see, the power coils that keep the pumps going are running down. Karvisian officials say that the first of them will go in a matter of weeks—maybe days. A couple of months from now, the pumps will grind to a halt for lack of power."

"Too bad," Quark remarked. "But I still don't see how—"

"My friend is one of the administrators of Karvis," she interrupted. "He recently learned of a supply of Cardassian power coils—just the kind his city needs. But they're owned by a Retizian, who wants to charge Karvis two arms and a leg for them."

Quark's eyes narrowed. "A Retizian, you say?"

The major nodded. "And not just any Retizian. This particular one got into a tough spot once upon a time, and needed the help of a Ferengi to get him out of it. In fact, you might say the Ferengi saved his life."

Quark's brow creased. "Fel Jangor," he muttered.

"I see you remember him," Kira noted. "Then you must also remember how you talked that Cardassian guard out of killing him—right here on this very station, if I'm not mistaken."

The Ferengi winced as he recalled the incident. "The Cardassian thought Jangor had insulted him. And of course, he had. But I hated to see such a clever businessman get killed for something so meaningless."

"A truly humanitarian gesture," the Bajoran remarked. "And one that could serve us all in good stead."

Quark looked at her. "You're asking me to take advantage of Jangor's debt to me?"

"I am," she said simply.

The Ferengi balked. "It wouldn't be right, Major."

"Since when does it disturb you to take advantage of people?" she asked.

"It's not that," Quark told her. "That kind of debt has real value, you know. I was saving it for a really big deal. How can I . . ." He searched for the right word. ". . . fritter it away on a bunch of strangers?"

"Strangers in desperate need of your help," Kira reminded him.

Quark shook his head. "I don't know," he said,

clearly on the fence about this. He grinned suggestively at her. "Unless, of course, you're absolutely *determined* to make it worth my while. . . ."

She knew what he was getting at. "Oh," she replied, "you'll get something for your troubles, all right."

His eyes lit up. Unconsciously, the fingers of his right hand rose to caress the lobe of his ear.

"I will?" he asked.

Kira grinned back at him. "Absolutely. You'll get an opportunity to continue doing business on *Deep Space Nine*." She ran her forefinger down the outside of his other ear. "Also, the undying admiration of this station's first officer, for a job well done."

The Ferengi sighed. "I have to admit, I'd hoped for a better deal. Maybe one with a quicker return on investment."

"Don't push your luck," she advised him, withdrawing her hand.

Quark muttered something uncomplimentary beneath his breath. "All right," he agreed, albeit with obvious reluctance. "I guess I have no choice in the matter. Count me in."

The major felt as if a terrible weight had been lifted from her shoulders. "That's good," she responded.

She was about to thank the Ferengi when she noticed something in his hands. It was round and blue, with a small hole in the top of it.

"By the way," Kira said, "what's that thing you're holding?"

The Ferengi looked down at it. He seemed surprised.

"Oh," he declared, turning away so that the thing was concealed from her, "it's nothing, really. Just some old family heirloom that Rom found in the storeroom. I was going to polish it and send it to my mother."

The major had a feeling he was going to do nothing of the sort. But, she mused, this wasn't a good time for Quark to be discovered committing a crime. At least, not until he was done helping Karvis.

Kira just smiled. "Whatever you say," she told him. Turning away, she left Quark's bar and its proprietor behind—secure in the knowledge that, one way or another, her friend would get his power coils.

CHAPTER
2

As CAPTAIN ISHIMAKI of the Federation *Starship* Zapata wove his way through the vessel's lounge toward his favorite table, he considered the quartet seated there.

The only familiar face was that of his first officer, Mara Klein. She fairly beamed at the sight of him.

Strange, the captain thought. Mara wasn't usually so glad to see him. After all, they'd had their differences lately. If she wasn't such a damned good exec, he might have been tempted to seek a transfer for her.

The others at the table peered at Ishimaki with muted curiosity—just about what he'd expected. It was only natural for a visitor to hold himself in reserve until he'd sized up his host. Obviously these three were no exception in that regard.

The first, he saw, was the Craynid—one of four in

the service of Starfleet, and the only female. There was no mistaking her hunched, vaguely insectoid posture, or her pale, almost translucent skin, or the round black eyes set into her massive head.

One of her companions was a Bolian, in the gold uniform of operations. The other was human, dressed in medical blue, with short brown hair that didn't draw enough attention from the length of her face.

"Well," said Ishimaki, as he stopped in front of his guests, "we meet at last. I apologize for not having been available to greet you personally as you arrived, of course—but there were extenuating circumstances."

Klein's smile actually broadened—something the captain wouldn't have thought physically possible. If he was mildly interested in her reaction before, now he was downright intrigued.

"It's all right, sir," his first officer told him. "I've already explained about our unscheduled side trip to Beta Jalonis, and how long you'd been without sleep."

"Believe me," remarked the Bolian, "we've all answered our share of colony distress calls. There's no need to make excuses."

Ishimaki inclined his head—a gesture of respect. "I appreciate that, Lieutenant. Zar, isn't it?"

The Bolian nodded congenially. "Tactical officer on the *Crazy Horse*. At your service."

Had Zar been human, the captain would have extended his hand. But to a Bolian, he knew, the gesture had no meaning.

Instead, he turned to the Craynid. "And you must

be Lieutenant Commander Graal," he concluded. "Chief engineer of the *Charleston,* I believe?"

The Craynid nodded her cumbersome head. "Correct," she rasped softly.

Finally he regarded the last of the visitors. And this time, he *did* extend his hand, since she was a fellow human.

For a moment, however, the woman failed to respond to the gesture. She stared at his hand, inspecting it as if it were some exotic variety of alien fauna. Finally she grasped it with her own.

Her touch was cold and a little clammy. But it was also brief.

"Dr. Laffer," Ishimaki noted.

"Yes," she replied simply.

Suddenly Klein got to her feet. "Sorry to leave so abruptly," she said, taking in the visitors with a glance, "but someone's got to be up on the bridge while the captain makes you feel at home. See you."

As she brushed past Ishimaki, he tried to divine the reason for his first officer's sudden departure. Despite her claim, there wasn't anything on the bridge that required her immediate attention. If she'd wanted to, she could have stayed a bit longer.

So, clearly, she hadn't wanted to. The captain wondered why.

First the inexplicable smile, then the sudden desire to be gone. One would think these people had been torturing Klein with Klingon painstiks.

Dr. Laffer leaned forward. "Captain?"

"Yes?" he answered.

"I hope you weren't thinking of calling me Miriam," she said. "Because I much prefer Dr. Laffer."

Ishimaki regarded her, thinking she was joking at first. Then, when he saw the way she looked back at him, he wasn't so sure.

"Dr. Laffer it is," he agreed, just in case.

"Good," said the doctor, with apparent earnestness.

The Bolian's mouth crept up at the corners. The captain got the distinct impression that he was trying to keep from laughing.

Ishimaki considered Laffer again, then Zar, then the Craynid. He smiled. "Am I missing something here?"

"Missing?" echoed Graal.

The captain nodded. "A joke, perhaps?"

"I don't make jokes," the doctor noted.

Ishimaki believed it. He was beginning to get an inkling of why his first officer had been so eager to leave.

"So," he began, trying to jump-start the conversation, "I guess you're all excited about the chance to christen the new *Saratoga?*"

"Yes," the Craynid hissed.

Of course, to the captain's mind, she didn't sound very excited. Nor did she look very excited. For all he knew, she was being sarcastic. It was difficult to tell on the basis of a one-word answer.

"Graal's not much of a conversationalist," Laffer pointed out.

Ishimaki believed *that* as well.

"We *are* excited," Zar chimed in. "Not that it makes up for the loss of the original *Saratoga*, of course. Or the deaths of the brave and dedicated people we served with."

"That is correct," the Craynid verified.

"On the other hand," Zar continued undaunted, "we worked hard to make the *Saratoga* the best ship in the fleet. It's good to know all that hard work didn't go unnoticed."

"Rest assured," said Ishimaki, "we'll get you to *Deep Space Nine* as quickly as possible. Then you can—"

"When do we eat?" interrupted Dr. Laffer.

The captain looked at her. "Eat?"

"Yes," said the doctor. "Eat. Ingest. Consume."

There was no irony in her voice—at least none that Ishimaki could detect. It was as if she honestly didn't think he knew what the word meant.

The captain had the feeling again that he was missing something. It was either that, or Laffer was the rudest human being he'd ever met.

"We can eat any time you like," he responded.

"How about now, then?" asked the doctor.

"Now is fine," Ishimaki told her.

Looking around, he spotted a waiter—a large, fair-haired man named Soderholm. He gestured.

A moment later, Soderholm was standing beside their table. "What can I get you?" the waiter inquired cheerfully of Ishimaki and his companions.

"Anything," Graal replied. "As long as it is Craynid food."

28

Soderholm glanced at the captain.

"It's all right," Ishimaki told him. "I had McCall program the replicator for several popular Craynid dishes."

"Any one will do," Graal whistled.

Soderholm shrugged. "Whatever you say, sir." He looked to Zar. "And what can I get for you, Lieutenant?"

"Anything that's *not* Craynid food," the Bolian replied. He grimaced good-naturedly. "When you see it, you'll understand."

The captain could only imagine. "All right, then. Lieutenant Zar and I will have the Actuman ginger chicken," he instructed the waiter. "And don't skimp on the seaweed." He turned to Laffer. "And you, Doctor?"

The woman waved her hand in front of her. "Nothing for me," she said.

Ishimaki regarded her. Laffer returned the scrutiny.

"Nothing?" he repeated. "Excuse me, but didn't you ask just a moment ago when we could eat?"

The doctor thought for a moment. "Yes," she said finally. "As a matter of fact, I believe I did."

The captain glanced at the waiter, who seemed somewhat perplexed now as well. Then he turned back to Laffer. "But now you're saying you don't want anything," he pressed.

"I don't," she explained. "I'm not hungry. I had something in my quarters just a little while ago."

He shook his head helplessly. "Then why did you ask about eating?" he inquired.

Laffer shrugged. "I don't know. Curiosity, I suppose."

"The doctor isn't all that enamored of dining in public," Zar interjected. "It's one of her quirks." He leaned forward and winked at Ishimaki. "One of her *many* quirks."

"I do *not* have quirks," Laffer insisted. "I have unique behavior patterns. And exemplary ones, at that."

"You are incorrect," stated the Craynid. "You have quirks."

The doctor's eyes narrowed. "Stuff it, Graal."

Soderholm grunted. "I think I'll get your orders now, Captain." With that, he whirled and made his escape—much as Ishimaki would have liked to.

Zar sighed and looked apologetically at the captain. "It was only a matter of time," he observed. "Usually, they go at it in the first thirty seconds."

Ishimaki steeled himself. From all appearances, it was going to be a very interesting evening.

Mara Klein would pay for this, he resolved. Oh, how she would pay.

First Officer Zina Forrest of the *Starship Agamemnon* was not an impulsive woman. She was not given to indiscretions of any kind, major or minor.

But as she and her companion turned the corner of a corridor and headed for the *Agamemnon*'s primary transporter room, Forrest was on the verge of committing the indiscretion to end all indiscretions.

The doors to the transporter room were just up ahead, not more than ten meters away. She would reach them in a matter of seconds.

Turning to the man beside her, whose blue and black uniform marked him as a Starfleet science officer, she studied his features for a moment. The large, soulful eyes, set beneath mysterious dark brows. The clean, well-defined jawline. The tousled black hair and the expressive lips.

In one moment, the man seemed the epitome of boyish innocence—full of mischief and a thirst for exploration. In the next, he appeared to know all that could possibly be worth knowing.

Suddenly, Forrest grabbed her companion by the shoulder, spun him around, and pinned him hard against the bulkhead. Then she kissed him full on the mouth, as passionately as she'd ever kissed anyone.

He didn't protest, either. He returned the kiss. And when she released him, a few moments later, she saw that his eyes were smiling at her.

She smiled too. "I'm going to miss you, Esteban Lopez."

His expression turned rueful. "I'll miss you too," Lopez assured her. "But the *LaSalle* frequents many of the same space routes as the *Agamemnon*. With any luck, we'll see each other again sometime soon."

"And if not," she said, "there are always shore leaves."

"Yes," he replied, running his fingers through her honey-colored hair. "There are always those."

He glanced about, as if he'd just remembered the circumstances. Fortunately, there was no one else in the corridor.

"We should continue to the transporter room," he advised gently, though there was a reluctance in his voice. "If anyone should see us like this . . ."

He was right, of course. Releasing him, Forrest stepped back and straightened the front of her tunic. Her lover did the same.

Then, as if nothing had taken place between them, either just then or over the last few days, they negotiated the remainder of the corridor and walked through the transporter room doors.

Tanya Federovna, the petite, pale-blonde ensign on duty, was attending to some last-minute adjustments at her control console. She barely looked up as the first officer joined her, or as their visitor crossed the breadth of the room on his way to the transporter platform.

Forrest's heart skipped a beat as she watched Lopez step up onto the platform and turn to look at her. Then he dutifully lifted his sculpted chin and looked away.

"Ready to transport," said Federovna.

"Energize," the first officer commanded, still hungrily taking in the sight of her paramour.

A moment later, Lopez was claimed by the transporter effect. And a moment after that, he was gone. Forrest sighed.

"You know," she said out loud, her judgment still

impaired by the man's spell, "men like him aren't easy to find."

"No," agreed Federovna, with equal fervor. "They're—"

Abruptly they looked at each other. The ensign looked surprised—shocked, even. Before Forrest's eyes, she turned a ripe shade of crimson.

"My god," said the first officer, doing her best to adjust to the situation. "Not you, too?"

A little sheepishly, Federovna nodded. "But I thought I was the only one." She winced. "How long . . . ?"

"Long enough," Forrest remarked.

She looked to the empty transporter platform, not quite sure how to feel about this. For a moment, she leaned toward anger. Then bitterness. But in the end, a smile came to her face.

"That bastard," she said admiringly. "That handsome, charming, silver-tongued bastard."

And she wondered if Lopez had made any *other* conquests while he was at it.

As Esteban Lopez materialized in the primary transporter room of the *Endeavor,* he mentally added the *Agamemnon* to the list of starships on which he was no longer welcome.

Too bad, he thought. All three of his romances there were quite stimulating, each in her own way.

Fortunately for him, there were plenty of other ships in the fleet, and plenty of attractive women who hadn't heard of him yet. And one of them, he noted happily, was standing behind the transporter console.

He was just about to make the woman's acquaintance when the doors to the room slid open. A bear of a man swaggered in, his small blue eyes blazing over his ample, golden brown beard.

What's more, Lopez knew this man. His name was Aidan Thorn, and he had once been the chief of security on the *Starship Saratoga*. Beyond that, he had been the science officer's closest friend.

"Esteban!" cried Thorn.

Lopez came down off the platform and extended his hand. The security officer nearly tore it off at the wrist in his exuberance.

"Yeow!" cried Lopez, clutching his forearm with his left hand. "Take it easy, damn you!"

"Fat chance of that!" roared the big man, wrapping Lopez in a bear hug that made the science officer's ribs ache. He couldn't even shout for mercy. He could only bear the pain until it was over.

Finally his tormentor set him free. Gasping for air, Lopez held his hand out, palm out for peace.

"No more," he breathed. "I may've survived the Borg, Thorn, but you'll be the death of me yet."

The big man grinned and brushed imaginary dust from his mustard and black tunic. "Come on," he gibed. "I took it easy on you. If I'd really wanted to hurt you, you'd be on your way to sickbay about now."

Lopez smiled. "How have you been, you old devil? How are things on the *Gorkon?*"

Thorn, who was in truth just a year older than Lopez himself, shrugged his big shoulders. "They're secure," he said, "which is how we security chiefs like it."

Over Thorn's shoulder, the science officer saw the transporter room doors slide apart again. He couldn't help but notice the form they admitted—a female one, and rather comely at that.

Dark skin, dark eyes, even darker hair. Her lips were full and inviting, her build lithe and athletic-looking. Yes, thought Lopez, very comely indeed.

Thorn turned to look in the same direction—and made a beckoning motion with his arm. "Come on, Counselor—don't be shy. This is the man I was telling you about—the one you and all the other ladies have got to watch out for, if you know what's good for you."

Lopez cursed inwardly. Leave it to his old friend Thorn to spoil his prospects. Not that it made things impossible for him, of course. Just a lot more difficult.

"I'm Esteban Lopez," he said cordially, inclining his head as he came forward to meet the counselor. "And you are . . . ?"

"Constance Barnes," the woman replied. "I work here." Her tone was detached, professional. And her expression only served to reinforce the impression. "Welcome to the *Endeavor,* Lieutenant Lopez."

The science officer smiled. "It's a pleasure to meet you, Counselor Barnes."

The woman's attitude changed a bit, then, though

Lopez couldn't have said exactly how. She cleared her throat.

"Obviously," she said, "you don't remember me, Mr. Lopez."

The science officer was caught off balance. He peered more closely at Barnes, hoping like crazy this wasn't one of his former liaisons come back to haunt him.

But try as he might, he didn't recognize her. Finally he cast a look at Thorn, who just grunted.

"I served with you on the *Saratoga,*" the counselor revealed at last. "Of course, I was only a trainee back then, and I'd only just arrived when the ship was deployed to Wolf Three-five-nine and our encounter with the Borg. You and I never had a chance to be formally introduced."

Lopez thought for a moment. "Yes," he said at last. "I do remember you now." It was a lie, of course.

Barnes shook her head. "No, you don't. I can tell. I'm a counselor, remember?"

For once, the science officer was speechless. Thorn seemed to find amusement in the fact.

"There's no need to massage my feelings," the woman pointed out. "I take no offense at not being remembered. And if it's any consolation, Mr. Thorn had no recollection of me, either."

"True," the security chief confirmed.

"Nonetheless," said Lopez, "I regret the fact. And I would like to make it up to you, somehow. Perhaps, with dinner?"

Barnes cracked a smile, at last. "Dinner?" she echoed.

He nodded. "We've got a while before we reach *Deep Space Nine.* Being old comrades, we might as well get to know each other."

"I don't think I'll have time for that," the counselor told him. "After all, I'm not a guest like you and Mr. Thorn here. I'm a member of the crew. And I've got a lot of work to finish before I can attend the Utopia Planitia ceremony in good conscience."

"But surely, you have to eat," Lopez entreated.

"Yes," Barnes agreed. "Unfortunately, it'll have to be at my desk." She paused. "Again, welcome to the *Endeavor,* Lieutenant. Mr. Thorn can show you to your quarters."

And with that, she turned and left the two men standing there, along with the transporter operator. Lopez turned to the young woman—a slender brunette with skin like alabaster.

"It appears I'll be free for dinner," he said. "I don't suppose you know where I can find someone to take the counselor's place."

The transporter operator regarded him sternly. "I'm on duty," she told him. Suddenly, her eyes crinkled playfully at the corners. "But I'm sure I'll be hungry when I get off."

Lopez grinned. "Excellent. I'll meet you here at the end of your shift. Deal?"

The woman nodded. "Deal," she agreed.

Good, thought Lopez, as he followed his friend

Thorn out of the transporter room. He wasn't sure he could have taken two rejections in the space of a single minute.

"You haven't changed a bit," the security chief noted, his eyes narrowed with obvious amusement.

"Nor have you," the science officer jabbed back. "Still trying to sink my ship before I get it afloat."

Thorn clapped him on the shoulder with a large, heavy paw. "Relax, Esteban. You would've struck out with Counselor Barnes no matter what."

"What makes you say that?" asked Lopez.

The bearded man shrugged. "I've been on the *Endeavor* for two days now, and I wasn't able to get so much as a smile out of the woman." He shook his head. "Not exactly the kind of personality one would expect from a ship's counselor, now is it?"

Lopez chuckled. "No," he agreed. "Come to think of it, it isn't."

CHAPTER
3

CAPTAIN NIKOLAS KYPRIOS shaded his eyes and scanned the mighty copper-colored disk of a sun. It was nowhere near its zenith yet, but it still dominated the purplish blue heavens of Danula II, and baked his leathery brown skin in a way the Greek sun never had.

Beneath that torturous sun and sky, the landscape was a flat, parched plain in every direction except south. As one gazed in the direction of the planet's distant equator, one saw the tawny, humpbacked hills that had broken many a runner's spirit.

But then, the Academy wouldn't have held their annual marathon here if the setting were too idyllic. The idea was to separate out the cadets with real grit, with real courage—not to pass a pleasant afternoon.

Of course, it had been thirty years since Kyprios

had run the *real* Academy marathon. This was just a holodeck re-creation, in which he took part once a month to keep himself sharp.

Planting his hands on the ground, Kyprios extended his right leg behind him and stretched out his calf muscle. Then he did the same with his left leg. Rising again and spreading his legs out, he reached for the dry, cracked ground with his palms, feeling his hamstrings strain in the process.

Only when he felt he was good and loose did he add the final ingredient, reluctantly yielding up his solitude. "Computer," he said, "add cadets."

A moment later, he found himself surrounded by young men and women of various races and planetary origins. Naturally there was no need for them to warm up. They were composed of magnetic fields, not real muscles.

The first few times he'd run this program, he'd raced through the hills all by himself. But after a while, he'd found the exercise lacking in stimulation. Kyprios had craved company—competition. Hence, the addition of the other runners into the mix.

The starting line was a shallow furrow cut into the ground. As one, the runners gravitated to it, Kyprios himself among them.

An Academy proctor he'd known—a small, muscular man named Tarleggia, who'd taught him quantum mechanics—approached the assembled competitors. Raising his hand, he alerted them to the imminence of the start.

The runners tensed, their eyes narrowed with purpose, their muscles taut with anticipation. Kyprios watched Tarleggia, eager to take off at precisely the moment his old instructor dropped his hand.

But before that could happen, a portion of the horizon disappeared in the shape of the holodeck entryway, and another flesh-and-blood person entered the program. The captain straightened.

"Freeze program," he commanded.

Immediately the other cadets froze in place, their bodies leaning, their eyes fixed on what they imagined to be the distant finish line.

Kyprios eyed the interloper. "I was wondering what had happened to you," he said.

Counselor Barnes frowned. "Sorry, sir. I had to file a few reports, and I lost track of the time."

The captain smiled forgivingly. "You've been doing that a lot lately, Constance. In fact, ever since this Utopia Planitia thing came up. Now, you could tell me that's a coincidence, of course—but I'd have a hard time believing it."

Barnes looked away, as if she'd suddenly developed an interest in the other runners. She sighed. "No," she said finally, in a low voice. "It's not a coincidence."

Kyprios eyed her. "That's why I asked you to meet me here, Constance. I'm concerned about how you're taking all this—the arrivals of your fellow officers, the prospect of seeing even more of them. Of revisiting an understandably traumatic time of your life." He paused. "We've never spoken much about what happened on the *Saratoga*."

"That's true," the woman admitted, still intent on the other runners. "We haven't."

"Would you like to talk about it now?" he asked.

The counselor turned to him, her dark eyes full of pain for a moment. Then the pain seemed to subside.

"The *Saratoga* was a bad experience," she said. "As bad as you may have imagined, and then some. All those people dying, and nothing—there was nothing I could do about it. I'd made it my life's work to help people, to ease their pain. But in a situation like that . . ."

"I know," the captain told her. "A counselor is of little or no use in those circumstances. Sparks flying, bulkheads exploding, alarms going off all over the place. It's all you can do to keep your wits about you."

Barnes sighed again. "You think you're prepared for it. At least, that's what they tell you they're doing at the Academy—preparing you for it. But you can't ever be ready for something like that."

Kyprios didn't want his ship's counselor to have to relive that kind of pain. He said as much.

"They'd miss you at Utopia Planitia," he told her. "But the hell with them. I'll cover for you."

Barnes shook her head. "No," she said. "I'm fine. In fact, in a funny way, I'm looking forward to it. If nothing else, it'll give me a sense of . . ." She shrugged. "Of closure, I guess."

The captain nodded. "If that's how you honestly feel about it, all right. But remember, you can always change your mind."

"Thank you," she told him, smiling just a little.

"But I don't think I'll need to do that. And in the meantime, I promise I'll try to lighten up a little."

Kyprios smiled. "You do that. Dismissed, Counselor."

Barnes retreated from the holodeck. The captain watched her go. And he didn't stop thinking about her until long after the irregularly shaped doors had interlocked behind her.

Sisko was just sitting down behind his desk when Dax's melodious yet efficient voice filled his office. "Benjamin, the *Zapata* has arrived. Captain Ishimaki is hailing us."

The captain turned to his Cardassian monitor, a vestige of the station's former occupants. "Open a channel, Lieutenant. And clear a space for the *Zapata* on the docking ring."

"Aye, sir," came the accommodating reply.

A moment later, Ishimaki's image appeared on the monitor. The face looked familiar, though Sisko had no idea where they might have met. He'd encountered so many officers in the course of his career, they'd all begun to blur a long time ago.

"Captain Sisko," said Ishimaki. "A pleasure to see you again."

The man really seemed to mean it. What's more, Sisko had a fair idea why that might be.

"Likewise," he answered. "As I understand it, you've been kind enough to bring some of my old comrades with you."

"I've got them, all right," said Ishimaki, stoically

43

avoiding the issue of just how kind he'd been. "But, as much as I've enjoyed their company, I'm going to have to turn them over to you."

Sisko noted a sense of relief on the man's part—a relief he well understood, having served with Laffer and Graal for a number of years. Still, he couldn't resist pushing a few of Ishimaki's buttons.

"Actually," he said, "we're having a bit of trouble with some of the airlocks on our docking ring. You may have to hang on to those old comrades of mine for another day or so until we get things worked out."

Ishimaki's eyes opened wide. With *fear,* Sisko thought. Somehow, he managed to keep a straight face.

"I know it's not your custom to beam people back and forth," said the captain of the *Zapata,* "but we'll have to make this an exception. After all, we've got pressing business . . . um, somewhere else."

Sisko smiled. "I'm sure you do, Captain. In that case, Lieutenant Dax will be glad to give you the coordinates of—"

"She needn't bother," Ishimaki assured him. "My transporter operator's identified an appropriate space for their arrival."

"I see," said Sisko. He leaned forward. "In that case, thanks for your help, Captain."

"Think nothing of it," Ishimaki answered. He was gone almost as soon as the last word was out of his mouth.

Turning to Ops, which was visible through his office

doors, Sisko noted the materialization of three figures to one side of Dax. Getting up, he circumnavigated his desk and walked outside.

There was some confusion among his station officers as to how and why the newcomers had shown up the way they did. However, thought Sisko, he'd take care of that in a moment.

"Zar!" he called out.

The Bolian turned to look at him. A grin spread over his face.

"Commander," he said warmly.

"Captain," Sisko corrected. With pure affection, he reached out and grasped Zar by the shoulder. "Good to have you aboard, Lieutenant."

The Bolian inclined his head. "Thank you, sir."

Sisko turned to the doctor. "Welcome to *Deep Space Nine,* Dr. Laffer. And don't worry—I have no intention of addressing you as Miriam, even if we have known each other for several years now."

Laffer nodded. "Good," she said. "I'm glad to hear that."

Finally, the captain addressed the Craynid. "Lieutenant Commander Graal. It's an honor to have you here."

As always, he treated the engineer with great deference. After all, she might have been his subordinate on the *Saratoga,* but she was a very high-ranking individual in her homeworld culture.

Graal looked at him askance. "Facial hair," she observed, "and you've shaved your head."

Sisko nodded. "Yes. You like it?"

The Craynid shrugged. "It is only hair," she remarked.

The captain smiled. He had missed Graal's unique perspective.

"Let me introduce you to my senior staff," he said.

With a gesture, Sisko indicated the people on whom he depended most these days. In accordance with his orders, they were all present on the bridge, assembled around Dax's station.

"This is Major Kira Nerys, my first officer. Major, Lieutenant Zar, Commander Graal, and Dr. Laffer . . . all old friends and colleagues from my days on the *Saratoga*."

Kira nodded. "A pleasure," she noted.

"And Lieutenant Dax—"

"The Trill," commented Laffer, her voice flat and inflectionless.

"Yes," replied Dax, sweetly enough. "I remember you, too, Doctor."

Unfortunately, their interactions hadn't always been congenial. Curzon Dax, her previous host, had time and again rubbed Laffer the wrong way. But then, Curzon had been a fun-loving sort, and the doctor was anything but.

"As you can see," the captain pointed out, "Lieutenant Dax—Jadzia to her friends—shares only *some* of Curzon's personality traits."

"That's good," remarked Zar. "Because I could never beat *Curzon* Dax at dom-jot. Maybe I'll have more luck with *Jadzia*."

The Trill shrugged. "You're welcome to try," she chuckled.

Clearing his throat, Sisko continued with his introductions. "Dr. Bashir, our chief medical officer."

Bashir smiled his most charming smile. "I've been looking forward to meeting you," he told their guests. "The captain has told us a great deal about you."

Not quite true, Sisko mused. But it was the polite thing to say. And Bashir seldom missed an opportunity to be polite.

"And last," the captain said, "but certainly not least, our hardworking chief of operations—Miles O'Brien."

O'Brien, who had a tool in each hand, just shrugged. "Sorry about that," he apologized, "but I was working on some Cardassian circuitry. I dream of the day when we've replaced it all with good, old Federation equipment."

Zar turned to Sisko. "What about your chief of security? The shapeshifter I've heard so much about?"

The captain grunted. "You'll meet Constable Odo in due time, Lieutenant. He would have been here as well, except he had some . . . how did he put it? Some official *business* to take care of."

Odo leaned over the bar, until his nose was almost touching Quark's. The Ferengi swallowed—hard.

"What did I do *now?*" protested Quark.

"Now," said the changeling, in a reasonable tone, "you've made communications contact with an individual known as Fel Jangor. A Retizian, whose dealings outside the law are almost as well known as your own."

Odo leaned back and pretended to admire his reflection in the polished surface of the bar. While the reflection itself was nearly perfect, the object it reflected was eminently flawed.

Despite all his skills at shapeshifting, he had never entirely mastered the humanoid form. As a result, his features looked rough, as if his maker hadn't quite finished with him.

Odo looked up again at the Ferengi. "Of course, you could deny it all. Then I would have to drag you back to my office, where I would show you proof of your communications. Or you could save us both some time and trouble and simply sever your dealings with Fel Jangor."

Quark sighed. "I can't," he said.

"Can't?" echoed the changeling. "And why not?"

The Ferengi looked more uncomfortable than Odo had seen him in a long time. "I can't tell you out here," he replied. He tilted his head in the direction of a shadowy corner table. "Grab me and pull me over there."

The shapeshifter looked at him. "You want me to *grab* you?" he asked.

"Yes," Quark whispered. "Come on. You want to know what's going on, don't you?"

Indeed, Odo *did* wish to know what was going on. Grasping the Ferengi by his upper arm, he guided him past the end of the bar and over to the table he'd indicated. Then he thrust Quark into a chair and pulled another one out for himself.

"All right," the constable went on, in a vaguely threatening tone, "here we are. What is it you were going to tell me?"

The Ferengi cast a few surreptitious glances about, to make sure they wouldn't be overheard. Then he leaned closer to Odo.

"I didn't want my altruism to become public knowledge," he explained. "It'd be bad for business. But, you see, I'm only speaking with Fel Jangor on behalf of Major Kira."

The shapeshifter looked at him. "You expect me to believe that?"

"It's true," Quark insisted. "The major asked me to obtain some power coils Jangor has in his possession. There's a village on Bajor in dire need of them. A place called Karvis."

"Why can't the village obtain the power coils itself?" Odo inquired. "Why do they need you?"

"Because the village can't afford them," the Ferengi explained.

"But you can," the constable concluded.

"That's right. You see, I did Jangor a favor some time ago. Kira believes I can trade on that favor to get the power coils cheaper."

Odo peered at Quark through narrowed eyes. "And can you?"

The Ferengi shrugged. "All I can do is try." He held his hands out. "So? Do you believe me now?"

The changeling didn't say anything. He was still

thinking about it, still searching Quark's features for a sign of dissembling.

"I'm as innocent as a newborn babe," the Ferengi advised. "Check with Kira if you don't believe me."

Odo frowned. "That won't be necessary," he said. "Clearly, you're telling the truth for a change."

"Good," replied Quark.

He got up to go, but the constable stopped him. The Ferengi looked exasperated.

"What?" he asked. "I thought we agreed that I was legitimate this time."

Odo shook his head from side to side. "Not at all. While I sympathize with the Bajorans' problems, I still can't let Fel Jangor dock his vessel at *Deep Space Nine*—or I'd be forced to seize it in accordance with the several warrants out for his arrest."

"Don't worry," Quark told him. "We weren't planning to conduct our business on the station, anyway. After all, you're not the only one who knows about those warrants." He smiled in appreciation of his own talents. "We've agreed to meet on a world in the next star system. That way, we can both be sure of avoiding interference as we pursue a transaction."

The changeling made a sound of disgust. "I don't need to know all the details," he declared. "Just that you'll be out of my jurisdiction."

"Which we will be," the Ferengi maintained.

"Which you'd *better* be," Odo remarked.

With a last withering glance, he got up and left Quark to his dealings. Despite the Ferengi's claims to the contrary, he had a nagging feeling he would live to regret all this.

With an effort, Miles O'Brien managed to dislodge the heavy bulkhead plate that covered the Cardassian power waveguide outlet. Casting a glance back over his shoulder, he smiled as best he could.

"If you don't mind, ma'am, I need you to step back. This plate is heavy, and I've got to put it down somewhere."

Lieutenant Commander Graal just looked at him for a moment, her dark eyes glistening in the rounded terrain of her alien skull. Finally, as if his request had taken a while to register, she moved back a couple of steps.

With a pronounced grunt, O'Brien lowered the bulkhead plate to the deck, careful not to lose his grip on it. Once before, shortly after he'd arrived on the station, he'd allowed a similar monstrosity to slip out of his hands.

It hadn't damaged the deck much, but he'd crushed a few toes. The pain had been excruciating. So if it took a little caution to avoid a repeat performance, that was the way it would have to be. He'd be as careful as a Cardassian with a tushpah egg.

"Well," he said, "there it is, Commander." Straightening, he indicated the exposed mechanism. "A Cardassian power waveguide outlet, in all its arcane glory—just as you requested."

Actually it had been Sisko's idea for O'Brien to

show the Craynid around the station, and to expose her to some Cardassian technology. But Graal hadn't objected when the offer was made.

"Of course," the human continued, "you'll notice the inefficiencies. And also, how damnably incompatible it is with Federation technology."

The Craynid inched forward again. Her eyes narrowed as she took in the sight. After a couple of minutes, she nodded.

"Yes," she hissed thoughtfully. "Inefficient and incompatible. But you say you incorporated it anyway?"

"That's right," O'Brien confirmed. "It wasn't easy, I don't mind telling you. But I found a way to modify our circuitry so that it accommodated Cardassian output. It was the only way I could convert the station without shutting it down and starting from scratch."

"I see," said Graal, still studying the waveguide outlet.

"Now, of course," the human went on, "we've got precious few of these things left. Almost every one of them has been replaced with an EPS conduit. But it took me a good few years to get to this point."

The Craynid turned to him. "With eighty-nine percent of rated power," she observed.

O'Brien frowned. "Eighty-eight percent, actually. But that was pretty good, I'd say, considering what I had to work with."

Graal shrugged. "You could have achieved ninety-two percent—perhaps as high as ninety-four."

The human looked at her. "Oh? And how's that?"

"By employing solid-state energy transfers," the Craynid explained.

O'Brien wasn't sure he'd heard her right. "Solid-state energy transfers haven't been used in almost forty years, Commander."

"True," Graal breathed. "But they are still stored in Starfleet distribution centers. And you would have found them to be much more compatible with a Cardassian power source."

The human thought about it for a moment. And the more he thought, the more he had to concede it wouldn't have been a bad idea.

Too bad he hadn't thought of it at the time.

The Craynid glanced at him. "I have seen all I wish to see. You may replace the bulkhead plate now."

O'Brien managed a semblance of a smile. "Of course," he replied. "Whatever you say, Commander."

Apparently, his sarcasm was lost on Graal. She didn't move a muscle as he bent down and hefted the bulkhead plate, or as he wrestled it back into place. Or as he grunted and cursed at the resulting twinge in his lower back.

It was only after he was finished, and was wiping the sweat from his brow, that she spoke again. "I would like to see a Cardassian transporter mechanism next," she told him.

The human shook his head. "We don't have those anymore. At least, not in working order."

"Then," the Craynid told him, "I would like to see one that is not in working order."

O'Brien looked at her and sighed. "Fine. It's in one of the cargo bays. Of course, I'll have to lug a few things around to get to it—assuming you don't mind that."

Graal regarded him. "No," she answered, seemingly oblivious to his implied protest. "I do not mind."

He bit his lip. "Very well, then," he told her, leading the way down the corridor. "This way, Commander."

The Craynid followed with that strange shuffling step of hers. Apparently she was warming to his little tour.

The captain would be pleased, O'Brien thought with a grimace. The only question now was which would give out first—Graal's curiosity or the chief's aching back.

CHAPTER
4

"As you can see," said Bashir, indicating the entire infirmary with a sweep of his arm, "we're not exactly embracing the state of the art out here. However, we manage somehow to get the job done."

Dr. Laffer nodded as she inspected the place, looking for all the world as if she were examining a patient with only a few days left to live. Abruptly the woman turned to him.

"You treated a Menas Baari here," she noted. "Didn't you?" She made it sound a bit too much like an accusation.

Bashir was certain she hadn't meant it that way. Well, he thought, relatively certain.

Of course, the Menas Baari *were* the scourge of the sector—amoral beings who made the Cardassians look benevolent. If they hadn't badly diminished their numbers with their incessant infighting, they might have been a bigger threat than the Dominion.

He shrugged. "Yes, I *did* treat a Menas Baari. And several thousand other patients, including a sprinkling of Ferengi, Cardassians, Klingons, In'taq, Pandrilites, Silesi, and even a Jem'Hadar—not to mention more Bajorans than you can shake a festival stick at."

Laffer frowned slightly. "It's the Menas Baari I'm interested in specifically. As I understand it, the patient was afflicted with Goryyn's syndrome. Pallid skin with raised green blotches, excess perspiration, soreness in the joints?"

Bashir smiled, though it didn't come easily. "I'm familiar with the symptoms," he told her. "And yes, I diagnosed the patient with Goryyn's. Fortunately, it wasn't the virulent kind."

"You had no trouble containing it, then?" she inquired.

Bashir found it a little harder to maintain his smile. "We do have forcefields here, Doctor. It really wasn't very difficult."

"And your cure?" she prodded.

He chuckled. This was all textbook stuff. "A steady diet of thoridium sulfide," he told her.

"Thoridium sulfide?" echoed Laffer. She looked away from him and shook her head. "Then you haven't seen Dr. Secori's monograph on Goryyn's?"

"Secori?" He shook his head. "I'm not familiar with the fellow."

His guest grunted in a vaguely derisive way. "Ainad

Secori of Muuldax Prime. He's on the cutting edge of immunology in the inner systems. I've met with him several times myself."

Bashir experienced a flare of resentment. Or was it a sudden sense of inferiority?

"And you're saying he's developed an alternative to thoridium sulfide?" he asked.

"That's correct," Laffer confirmed. "A substance called *benarrh*, derived from the stamen of the Muuldaxan *kras'suda* blossom. It has a ninety-eight-percent cure rate when introduced in the first two days."

That was six percent higher than anyone had achieved in the past. Bashir couldn't help but be impressed. But even more than that, he was annoyed.

How was it this Secori had come so far in this area and he'd never gotten wind of it? Was he really that isolated out here on *Deep Space Nine?* Or was his guest perhaps making more of the Muuldaxan's work than she ought to be?

"I'll have to look into it," he promised.

Laffer didn't respond to his comment. Instead she continued to scrutinize the infirmary—paying particular attention to his scalpel set, which was housed in a transparent plastic case.

"That was a gift," Bashir pointed out. "From my aunt Gauri and uncle Nigel. I received them when I graduated medical school."

"I see," said Laffer.

She didn't say the scalpels were antiquated. She didn't say they were ineffective. But there was something in her voice that implied those things nonetheless.

"They're really quite adequate," he added.

"I'm sure they are," Laffer replied.

She moved on toward his surgical alcove. Bashir tagged along, not at all eager to continue the tour—not that he had any choice. The captain had entrusted him with a former colleague, and he had to make the most of it.

Halfway to the alcove, Laffer stopped at his desk and reached for something. Surprisingly it was his racquetball trophy.

"First place," she noted, reading the information off the base of it.

He nodded. "Yes. I got lucky, I suppose. I hadn't even mastered the three-corner ceiling shot at that point."

Laffer turned to look at him. "But you've mastered it now?" she asked.

Bashir shrugged. "By now? I should say so. It's the most effective shot in my repertoire." He paused. "Do you . . . er, play?"

She shook her head. "No, I was never inclined much toward sports. Too hard on the joints. However, I have a friend who won the Starfleet Medical tournament back on Earth."

"Really?" He was impressed. "That wouldn't be Marta Grindberg, would it?"

"Actually," she replied, "it is."

Bashir smiled. "I'll bet *she* makes good use of the three-corner ceiling shot."

Laffer put the trophy down where she'd found it. "To tell you the truth, she never uses it. Not anymore, I mean."

He felt his jaw drop. "Why not?" he asked.

"I don't really know," his guest told him. "She just says it's out of fashion. None of the better players resort to it any longer."

Bashir felt his cheeks burning. "Oh," he responded lamely. "Well, that'll teach me to be so out of touch."

The woman's game was obvious to him now. She was the high priestess of one-upmanship, the ultimate contrarian. Whatever he'd done, she knew someone who'd done it better. Whatever he said, she had some counterargument waiting in the wings.

It might have been out of spite or jealousy. Or it might simply have been her nature.

In either case, if he was going to survive the remainder of this tour, he would do better to turn the spotlight somewhere else. In other words, on Laffer herself. And as luck would have it, there really was something Bashir had been meaning to ask her.

"Tell me something," he said, maneuvering himself into a position between Laffer and the surgical alcove.

She looked at him. "What would you like to know?"

He rubbed his hands together. "The Siskos—both the captain and Jake—have a rather interesting residue of cells in their blood." He went on to describe them.

"That's correct," Laffer confirmed. "They were left over from our exposure to a rather rare disease, during our time on the *Saratoga*. We all have those cells."

Bashir held his hands up, calling for a halt. "Actually," he said, "according to your medical records, two of you do *not* exhibit those cells. More specifically, Lieutenant Lopez and Counselor Barnes."

She frowned slightly. "And it's not clear to you why that should be."

"Let's say I'm a little curious about it," he pressed.

"The answer is a simple one," Laffer responded. "Neither Lieutenant Lopez nor Counselor Barnes were on the *Saratoga* when the crew encountered the disease. Lopez joined us very shortly afterward, and Barnes a full year later." She stared at him. "But this information is in their medical records. You *did* say you'd received them, didn't you?"

Bashir's cheeks burned even hotter than before. "Yes," he said, regretting his oversight. "I received them, all right. I just hadn't read them all the way through yet."

"Well," Laffer remarked, "if you had, you'd have seen that we contracted a rather dangerous strain of the disease. And that some of us, Commander Sisko included, were close to death when I discovered a cure."

She went on to give Bashir the details—many more of them, in fact, than he might have desired or found remotely useful. And just when he thought she was through, she went on to catalog several other instances in which she rescued the crew of the *Saratoga*.

Bashir sighed. He sorely wished he had never brought the subject up in the first place.

Sisko's laughter filled the upper level of the Promenade, attracting more than a couple of looks from passersby. He put his arm around his son's shoulders and shook his head.

"Dinner?" he echoed. "With both of them? At the same table?"

Zar, who was walking alongside them, smiled mischievously as he nodded. "Ishimaki just didn't know who he was dealing with. You should have seen his face when Laffer prodded him to call a waiter over—and then told him she'd already eaten."

"That poor man," said the captain. "Now I'm sorry I teased him a bit when he arrived with you three in tow."

The Bolian looked at him. "You teased him? By the deities, you should have given him a medal."

Sisko chuckled and turned to Jake. "Do you remember what those two were like together?" he asked.

The youngster shrugged. "I thought I did. I guess they didn't seem so bad to me—maybe because I didn't see them very much."

"Thank your stars," quipped Zar. "I wish I could have said the same."

"And now," the captain commented ruefully, "I've asked two of my most trusted officers—men I like—to baby-sit for Graal and Laffer. What kind of commanding officer am I?"

"You had no choice," the Bolian told him. "Laffer made a point of asking to see the infirmary. And Graal would have asked to see *something,* if you hadn't suggested it yourself."

Sisko sighed. "I suppose. Just remind me of that when O'Brien and Bashir stage a mutiny."

"Hey, Jake," said Zar. He pointed to an exotic foods emporium along the Promenade. "I'll bet they've got some mak'terama drops in there."

The boy smiled. "They do," he said. "Big ones. Three different flavors, too, each one better than the last." He sobered as he looked at his father. "But my dad says they're too sweet. They'll rot my teeth."

"Well," remarked the Bolian, assuming an equally sober mien, "in that case, there's just one thing to do." He cast a sidelong glance at Sisko and leaned closer to Jake. "We won't tell the old fellow."

Then, with a cackle, Zar hooked the boy by his arm and pulled him in the direction of the emporium. The captain watched them go, unable to keep from cracking a smile himself.

Undoubtedly, the Bolian was a bad influence. But he was a very *good* bad influence. Especially for Jake, who'd looked up to Zar like an older brother during their stint on the *Saratoga.*

Those were good times, Sisko reflected. Family times. And the Bolian had, for all intents and purposes, been part of their family.

He'd worshipped Jennifer in particular. Hadn't Zar said, time and again, that she'd spoiled him for other women? That he'd never settle down until he could find a mate as beautiful and bright and charming as Sisko's?

With all that, it couldn't have been easy for the Bolian to leave Jennifer behind on the *Saratoga*—to countenance her crushed and broken body, and pull her husband away from her. But Zar hadn't had any choice in the matter.

He had done what he had had to do. And ever since, Sisko had been grateful to the Bolian.

Except for the first few days, of course. During that time, the captain had hated him. With a passion. It was only after he'd had time to think about it that he realized what kind of favor Zar had done for him. If not for the Bolian, he would have been a dead man.

So if Zar wanted to spoil Jake a little, if he wanted to stuff him with those damned mak'terama drops, the captain would see fit to overlook the transgression. After all, the Bolian had earned it.

Abruptly, his communicator bleeped. He tapped it. "Sisko here."

It was Kira. "Sir," she said, "the *Endeavor* has arrived. We've directed it to docking pylon two."

The captain grunted by way of acknowledgment. "Thank you, Major. I'm on my way."

Kira's timing was good. By then, Jake and Zar were coming out of the exotic foods emporium with a couple of bags full to bursting. They were grinning from ear to ear—a sight that did Sisko's heart good.

"Come on," he called to them. "Hurry up, you two. It looks like the rest of our visitors have shown up."

* * *

As Captain Kyprios stood in the airlock, he glanced at Counselor Barnes, who had positioned herself on his right flank. He sought some hint of trepidation in her face, some indication that she had lied to him about her determination to take part in this Utopia Planitia thing.

But he perceived nothing of the kind. The counselor looked composed, even eager to be here.

Barnes was such a good officer, such a good friend, Kyprios hated the idea of letting her inflict pain on herself. If she had shown the slightest sign of distress, he would have found a reason to extricate her.

But there was no sign. And, therefore, no reason to pull her out.

Relax, he told himself. She's a grown woman. She knows what she's doing. He just wished he believed it.

Turning his head, he noted the presence of Thorn and Lopez on his other flank. If the counselor was looking forward to this, they were downright ecstatic. They hadn't stopped laughing and slapping each other on the back since Lopez's arrival.

Clearly this was a different kind of experience for them than it was for Constance Barnes. A *very* different experience. They had managed to put the tragedy behind them and move on.

The grinding of gears caught Kyprios's attention. Facing forward, he saw the Cardassian-style doors begin to part. He had a feeling he knew who would be on the other side.

The captain had never met Benjamin Sisko, though

he had heard a lot about him—even before the *Endeavor* played host to Thorn and Lopez. After all, the man had been in the eye of a mounting storm the last several years, and had comported himself better than anyone expected.

So as the docking-bay doors continued to slide apart, Kyprios confessed inwardly to a certain curiosity—a certain interest in the kind of man who could take a run-down relic of a station and make it a key piece on the galactic chessboard. A moment later, that curiosity was satisfied, as the aperture widened enough to reveal three figures.

One was a Bolian. Obviously not Sisko.

The second was much too young to be the station commander. Hell, he wasn't even wearing a Starfleet uniform.

It had to be the third one, then. The man with the clean-shaven head and the dark goatee, and the look of quiet confidence about him. And, of course, the command colors. Yes, that would be *him,* all right.

Kyprios took a couple of steps forward and extended his hand. "Captain Sisko, I presume?"

The station commander smiled cordially. "Captain Kyprios. Welcome to *Deep Space Nine.*" He nodded to his companions. "Lieutenant Zar of the *Crazy Horse.* And my son," he said, with an unmistakably paternal pride. "Jake."

The Bolian nodded. A little more hesitantly, betraying a typically teenage awkwardness, the youngster did the same.

"Pleased to meet you both," Kyprios told them. He turned to Sisko again. "I take it you know these three?" He indicated his companions with a tilt of his head.

Sisko's smile faltered a little. "Yes," he replied, "Lieutenant Lopez and Mr. Thorn are old friends."

"Bloody right we are," chuckled the security chief.

Lopez elbowed Thorn for his breach of protocol. "Mind your manners," he said. But he had trouble containing a smirk of his own.

"However," the station commander went on, ignoring the other two and gazing at Barnes, "I don't believe I knew Counselor Barnes very well."

"That's true," she remarked evenly. "I was new on the *Saratoga* when it was destroyed. But it's a pleasure to meet you now, sir."

Sisko inclined his head chivalrously. "The pleasure is mine, Counselor." He turned to Kyprios again. "Will you be staying on, Captain?"

Kyprios shook his head. "I'm afraid not. I just wanted to pay my respects—and to see in whose hands I'm leaving my ship's counselor."

"I'll take good care of her," Sisko promised.

"See that you do," said Kyprios, only half in jest. "I'll be back in a couple of weeks. Until then, sir."

"Until then," the station commander echoed.

Kyprios could see in his eyes that Sisko understood his concerns. Feeling a little better than he had when he arrived, the older man nodded to his counselor, turned about, and made his way back to his ship.

* * *

Sisko watched Kyprios depart. Certainly the man didn't pull any punches. He was concerned about his counselor and he didn't care who knew it.

"Pay no attention to my commanding officer," said Barnes.

Sisko looked at her. "I beg your pardon?"

She smiled apologetically. It was an attractive and strangely unexpected smile. "Captain Kyprios is known to overdo it sometimes. He's very protective of his people."

So am I, thought Sisko. But I don't show it that way. At least, I don't *think* I do.

"That's all right," he assured her. "I'm sure his heart is in the right place."

In the meantime, Zar and Jake were exchanging greetings with Lopez and Thorn. The big man picked Jake up like a baby—something Sisko himself hadn't attempted for a number of years now.

"You used to be such a pipsqueak," said Thorn. "Now look at you. You're bigger than Lopez."

"So he is," the science officer agreed. "I'll bet the ladies can't keep their hands off him."

Jake squirmed a bit under the scrutiny of his old shipmates. "Come on, guys. This is embarrassing."

"Let him down," said Sisko, intervening. "And as for the ladies," he added, casting a remonstrative glance at Lopez, "the last thing he needs is encouragement."

"That's right," Zar chimed in, affecting a fatherly demeanor. "He already spends more time with the Dabo girls than he does at his studies."

Barnes cleared her throat. Obviously she felt like a fifth wheel at this gathering.

"If someone will show me to my quarters," she told the station commander, "I think I'd like to call it a day."

Sisko nodded. "Of course. I'll see you there myself."

She held up her hand. "That won't be necessary," she told him. "I wouldn't want to pull you away from your reunion."

"No," said the captain. "I insist." He turned to Lopez and Thorn. "In fact, I'll show you *all* to your quarters. The reunion can wait until later, after I've taken care of some things."

The big man nodded understandingly. "Of course. You've got a station to run. You're busy."

Sisko grunted. "Unfortunately." He tilted his head to indicate the direction in which they would proceed. "This way."

As the captain led them along the corridor, his son and colleagues fell into line behind him. All except Lopez, who wound up walking beside him.

"Esteban," he said, taking advantage of the opportunity. After all, the others were conversing among themselves.

The science officer looked at him. "Yes?"

Sisko smiled. "You know what I'm going to say, don't you?"

Lopez shook his head, his eyes full of innocence. "No, what?"

Apparently Thorn had been listening in. He caught up with them in a couple of long strides.

"You're not to terrorize the females on the station," the bearded man provided. *"That's* what."

The science officer feigned indignation. "Me?" he replied. He shook his head. "You wrong me, Captain. I'm not nearly the bon vivant I used to be. I've mellowed in my old age."

"Sure you have," said Thorn.

Lopez cast a reproachful look at him. "Nothing like a character reference from a friend," he muttered.

Sisko chuckled. "Your cover's blown, Esteban."

"Don't worry," said the security chief. "I'll keep him on a short leash, Captain. He won't get into any trouble while I'm around."

"See that he doesn't," Sisko advised. "There are a great many temptations on this station. I'd hate to see an old comrade fall on the wrong side of a jealous husband."

"I hear you," Thorn assured him.

The science officer scowled resentfully at his powerful-looking friend. "Yes," he said. "And so did I."

"Good," the captain responded. "Then we won't have any misunderstandings." Satisfied that he had done his job, he headed for the Promenade.

CHAPTER
5

SHUTTING OUT THE sights and sounds of Quark's as he always did, Bashir tried to line up the dart in his hand with the round board on the wall. However, he couldn't seem to make himself concentrate this time.

"What's wrong?" asked O'Brien.

The doctor turned to him, exasperated. "Wrong?" he echoed. "Who said anything was wrong?"

The engineer recoiled a bit. "Sorry I asked," he responded. "You don't have to bite my head off, y'know."

Bashir bit his lip. "You're right, Chief. I didn't. I apologize. It's just that"—he looked around, to make sure there was no one in earshot—"that Dr. Laffer," he finished.

O'Brien looked at him. "Gave you some trouble, did she?"

The doctor grunted. "Not exactly, no. I mean, she didn't wreck the infirmary or anything. On the other hand, she made me feel about this small." He used the thumb and forefinger of his left hand to indicate a millimeter or so. "First she criticized my methods, then my equipment, and finally even my approach to racquetball. By the time she finished, I was seriously wondering if I was capable of doing *anything* right."

The operations chief chuckled mirthlessly. "Sounds nearly as bad as Lieutenant Commander Graal." He considered his own darts and frowned. "If she'd had me move one more piece of equipment, I'd be stretched out on one of your operating tables now—awaiting a spine replacement."

Bashir smiled at the notion. "You would have had to ask Dr. Laffer for one of those. I'm neither trained nor equipped for anything more complicated than a splinter removal."

His friend seemed as if he was about to say something more—but something distracted him. Following the engineer's gaze, the doctor saw what had snared O'Brien's attention.

It was Lopez, the science officer from the *LaSalle*. And he had just escorted Dax to a secluded table in the back of the place.

Bashir found his teeth grating together. He flung his dart at the board. It missed, embedding itself in the wall instead.

O'Brien grunted. "Feeling a little jealous, are we?"

The doctor glared at him. "Of what?" he inquired. "Jadzia is a grown woman. What she does with her time is her own business." He glanced again at Lopez, who was in the process of moving a little closer to the Trill. "Besides," he went on, "we're just friends."

"Er, right," the chief responded, lining up his shot. "Whatever you say, Julian."

He let the dart fly. It struck the bull's-eye dead on.

Bashir whirled on him, prepared to defend himself against O'Brien's suggestion. Then he stopped himself. What was the use? Some people were just more transparent than others, he supposed—and he was one of them.

"All right," he admitted. "Maybe I *am* a little jealous—in a brotherly sort of way. And a little puzzled, as well. I mean, I don't know what Jadzia *sees* in the man."

The engineer shrugged. "She must see something," he remarked. "Otherwise she wouldn't be sitting next to him."

He had barely gotten the words out when Dax excused herself, leaving Lopez all alone at the table. Bashir harrumphed, deriving a measure of satisfaction from the turn of events. It seemed his friend Dax had better taste than he had given her credit for.

"She's left him," O'Brien pointed out.

The doctor smiled. "Has she? I hadn't noticed."

"And by the looks of it, he's decided to visit us instead," the chief continued.

Bashir glanced over his shoulder. Sure enough, Lopez was headed their way, weaving his way through the crowd. The doctor frowned. What did the man want of them?

"Excuse me," said the science officer when he had gotten close enough. He smiled a rather disarming smile. "My name is Lopez. Esteban Lopez, science officer on the *LaSalle*. You know, one of Captain Sisko's muckety-muck friends from the *Saratoga*, come to disrupt things here and generally plague you until we finally depart for the commissioning ceremony?"

O'Brien laughed. Bashir couldn't help but chuckle a bit himself.

"I wouldn't say you were plaguing us," the engineer lied. "At least, not yet."

"Ah, then you haven't met Commander Graal yet," Lopez told him. "Or even worse, Dr. Laffer." He turned to the doctor. "Then again, judging by the grimace on your face, perhaps you have."

Bashir started to protest. "That was not a grimace. I—"

O'Brien put a comradely hand on his shoulder. "Give it up, Julian. The man has got us dead to rights." He addressed the newcomer. "How did you ever tolerate them on the *Saratoga?*" he asked.

Lopez shrugged. "I stayed away from them, mostly."

"Good advice," the Ops chief observed. "I'll have to remember that."

"Of course," said the science officer, "they're not the only ones you have to look out for. There's also my friend Thorn. The man doesn't know his own strength. Don't let him pat you on the back when he's had one too many, or there'll be a permanent impression of your face in the tabletop."

"I'll remember that, too," promised O'Brien, flinching a little at the image.

"And then there's me," Lopez went on. "Lock up your wives and daughters, Esteban Lopez is in town." He grinned. "And I must admit, I'm flattered by my reputation. I only wish it was quite as well deserved as some make it out to be."

"You mean it's not?" the doctor inquired casually.

"Oh, there's always a kernel of truth in every rumor." The science officer sighed. "But it's just a kernel, I'm afraid. As you no doubt noticed," he continued, "my efforts with Lieutenant Dax were quite futile. So, as you can see, I'm as fallible as anyone else."

Bashir grunted. "That's good to know."

Lopez looked at him. "Actually, as Dax tells it, you're the resident Romeo around here, Doctor. She even confessed to having a soft spot for you herself—though I'm sure that comes as no surprise to you."

"It doesn't?" responded Bashir. "I mean . . . no, of course it doesn't." He managed a smile. "What else did she tell you?"

The science officer looked at him apologetically. "I think, perhaps, that's all I should say. Bad enough I'm thought of as a gigolo, you understand. I don't want to be called a gossip into the bargain."

The doctor bit his lip. "I understand," he said.

It seemed that Lopez was more of a gentleman than

he had believed. The man's stock went up instantly in Bashir's eyes.

"So," said the science officer, tilting his head in the direction of the dartboard, "would you mind very much if I joined your game?"

The doctor and O'Brien looked at each other. Both men shrugged.

"Not at all," said the Ops officer.

"Be my guest," said Bashir.

O'Brien gestured to Rom, who was passing by with an empty tray. "Another round, please," he called out. He glanced at Lopez. "What can I get you, Esteban?"

"I'll have a beer," the science officer replied. "But let me get this round. It's my way of apologizing for my colleagues' behavior."

"I can't let you do that," O'Brien insisted, holding up a hand for emphasis.

"No," said Lopez firmly. "I insist. Really."

The Ops officer sighed. "Very well, then." He turned to Rom. "You heard the man."

The Ferengi nodded. "I'll put it on your tab," he told the science officer.

"Thank you," said Lopez. He turned to O'Brien. "Now, I warn you, I'm no pushover at this. There's a dartboard on the *LaSalle*, you know."

The doctor stifled a smile. "There are plenty of dartboards," he remarked. "But there's only one Miles O'Brien."

As it turned out, their visitor was pretty good. Not

as good as O'Brien, of course, but better than Bashir had expected.

And that wasn't the only way in which Lopez surprised the doctor. As they played, it became clear to Bashir that the science officer was a regular fellow—one who hadn't merited the doctor's jealousy in the least.

"Well," said Lopez, after he had come in third for the second game in a row, "it looks like Chief O'Brien isn't the only ringer around here." He clapped Bashir on the shoulder. "You're pretty good yourself, Doctor."

Bashir smiled. "Just lucky, I assure you."

Lopez looked at him with mischief in his eyes. "What do you say we make the game a bit more interesting?"

"In what way?" asked Bashir.

"Well," said the science officer, "we *could* make a little wager on the outcome. Even odds, winner takes all."

The doctor felt a bit uncomfortable at the suggestion. After all, he wasn't in the habit of gambling with friends. Hell, he wasn't in the habit of gambling with *anybody*.

Apparently the chief felt the same way. "I don't know," he replied, looking a little queasy. "I mean, I usually play just for fun."

"And a wager should make it *more* fun," Lopez suggested. "Unless, of course, you don't feel you can perform under pressure."

He had clearly found the right button to push—

O'Brien's pride. The chief laughed. "Don't feel I can perform?" he repeated. "I'll have you know I thrive under pressure."

"Then it's a bet," the science officer concluded. "One bar of latinum, or the equivalent."

"A bar of latinum?" O'Brien echoed. He winced a little. "That sounds like a lot of money."

Lopez chuckled. "There's no point in wagering unless it means something," he explained, then turned to Bashir. "Are you in, Doctor?"

Bashir didn't like the direction in which this was headed. He almost felt as if he were being coerced. And that feeling gave rise to an unwelcome thought.

What if Lopez were a con man? A hustler? What if he'd been lulling them into a false sense of security this whole time, hoping to take them for all they were worth—starting with a bar of latinum and going on from there?

The science officer smiled at him. "You're hesitating, my friend. That's a bad sign. It means you don't trust me."

The doctor flushed. "It's not that," he said.

"Then you're in," Lopez concluded. Perhaps too briskly, he turned to O'Brien. "And you, Chief?"

The Irishman shrugged. "I suppose," he replied.

"Good," said the science officer. "Let's give it a go, then, shall we? Three rounds a game?"

Bashir had the less-than-pleasant feeling that they had been hoodwinked. He could already feel himself a bar of latinum lighter.

As the first round of darts flew, the results were the

same as in the previous game. O'Brien opened a clear lead, with the doctor and Lopez neck and neck. A second round only saw the chief widen his lead. And in the third round Bashir snuck ahead of the science officer to take second place.

Lopez sighed. "Good game," he told his newfound companions. "Care for another, gentlemen? Say, for twice the stakes?"

The doctor swore inwardly. It was happening just as he had predicted. His less-than-pleasant feeling got a good deal worse.

"Not me," said Bashir. "I know when I'm outclassed."

The science officer glanced at him in a vaguely disappointed sort of way, then turned to O'Brien. "Looks like it's just you and me, Chief."

The doctor hoped his friend would decline as he had. But after a moment he could see that wasn't going to happen. It wasn't O'Brien's style to be a party pooper—or to imply, by dropping out, that he suspected Lopez of being a crook.

"Looks that way," the chief agreed, if a little reluctantly.

The second contest went much as the first one had. Of course, their guest couldn't have come in third this time, with the doctor out of the game. Still, the science officer's score was lower by ten points.

"Damn," he breathed, as he plucked his darts out of the board. "That's two bars of latinum I owe you," he told O'Brien.

The chief made a gesture of dismissal. "Listen, Esteban, you don't owe me anything. Let's just call it even, all right?"

Lopez shook his head. "I'm not a welsher, Chief. Give me one more shot. And we'll double the stakes again. That'll make it four bars of latinum."

O'Brien's lips became a thin hard line. Four bars of latinum was a lot of money. And as good as he was, there was always the chance he would falter—or that the newcomer would get lucky.

Bashir stared at his friend—hard. Don't do it, he thought. He's just reeling you in, Chief.

But O'Brien was too honorable a man to back out now. "Done," he told the science officer. "Four bars it is."

There was no fun in this game—for either man, the doctor thought. It was grim and tense and everything a friendly game of darts shouldn't be.

The first round went to Lopez. The chief had missed badly with his first dart, putting himself in a hole. And the science officer took advantage of it, coming up with what was easily his best performance so far.

The second round was O'Brien's, however. His eye seemingly sharpened by his failure in the first round, he placed all of his darts in and around the bull's-eye. Lopez did well, too, much better than he had done in their earlier matches—but not well enough.

The third round would decide it. The science officer turned to O'Brien. "How are you feeling, Chief?"

O'Brien nodded. "Not bad. And you?"

"Pretty confident, actually," said Lopez. "Confident enough to double the stakes again, if you've got the stomach for it."

He smiled, but not with any genuine feeling. It was the smile of a cat, Bashir thought, just before he made mincemeat of a poor mouse.

The chief looked drawn, hollow-cheeked. He swallowed. "Whatever you say," he told the science officer.

Inwardly the doctor winced. Eight bars of latinum? It would take his friend forever to make that kind of money.

But O'Brien had already agreed to the wager. His jaw set in grim concentration, he stared at the board and lined up his dart. Then he drew it back and, with a flick of his wrist, sent it flying end over end.

It embedded itself in the dartboard midway between the center and the edge. Not a terrible shot, but certainly not the man's best.

The next dart was in more or less the same spot. A thin rivulet of perspiration made its way down the side of O'Brien's face. Bearing down, he tossed the third dart—and stabbed the bull's-eye with it.

But he was vulnerable, and he knew it. Bashir sighed. He could feel his comrade's frustration and pain. How was he going to explain this to Keiko, after all? That he had lost all their savings and then some?

Lopez stepped up and lodged his first dart not far from O'Brien's, near the center. A smile tugged at the corners of his mouth—a smile which didn't go unnoticed by the doctor.

The science officer's second dart wasn't as well placed, however. It barely caught the perimeter, eliciting a muffled curse from the man. And his third toss missed the board entirely.

The game was O'Brien's. Bashir could see the chief breathe a sigh of relief.

Lopez, on the other hand, looked pale and waxy—almost feverish in his disappointment. At least, for a moment. Then, as the color returned to his face, he raised his eyes to O'Brien's and extended his hand.

"Looks like you've won," he noted, in a clear, steady voice. "I'll make arrangements to get you your winnings."

The chief shook his head. "There'll be no need," he said emphatically. "The competition was worth more to me than any amount of latinum."

But Lopez was just as insistent. "As I told you," he replied, "I'm not a welsher, Chief. See you later." He turned to Bashir. "And you, Doctor."

Bashir nodded, still a little stunned. He watched the science officer disappear into the crowd, then turned to O'Brien.

"I could have sworn he was going to hustle you," he muttered.

The chief managed a half-smile. "Yeah," he said. "Me, too. I guess neither one of us is much of a judge when it comes to character." He paused. "Of course, I can't let him pay me all that latinum."

"Of course not," the doctor agreed.

He still couldn't believe it. What kind of a man was this Esteban Lopez? What kind of a fool, to jack the stakes up that way . . . when he had every reason to expect he would lose?

Bashir shook his head. There were some things he would *never* understand.

CHAPTER 6

"THE IMPORTANT THING to remember," said Kira, as she moved her forefinger along the bright red schematic depicted by the tactical monitor, "is that the Cardassians didn't mind losing a few troops here if they could ultimately claim victory."

"I see," replied Zar, who was standing at her side in Ops.

"In fact," she went on, "they would generally rather lose a few troops than lose no troops at all, because—"

"Because if they didn't lose anyone," Zar interrupted, "it means they didn't fight very hard."

Kira looked up at him and smiled. "That's right. But I thought you didn't know much about Cardassians . . . ?"

"I don't," he confirmed. "But I've heard of other

83

races who thought the same way. After a while, you begin to see a pattern."

Kira nodded. "Yes," she said, "I suppose you do."

After all, Zar had been a tactical officer for a good many years. He would know these things.

A moment later, the major resumed her inspection of the grid. Where was that damned thing, anyway?

"Ah," she blurted after a moment. "Here it is."

She pointed out the Cardassian shield generator on the grid. It was the only one on this particular schematic, though there had been eleven others on the station.

Peering over her shoulder, the Bolian took it all in. "And it could simply be bypassed?" he asked. "Automatically?"

"That's right," she told him. "The shield generators were set up to draw power according to prevailing circumstances. The trigger was generally a percentage of rated strength. So if the station were under attack and shield strength dropped below, say, seventy-five percent . . ."

"Power was shifted away from the more expendable areas and directed to the operations center," Zar finished. "And of course, that's where the highest-ranking officers were holed up." He gestured to indicate Ops. "The shields around this facility were restored to full strength, while other parts of the station were left all but defenseless."

"Exactly." Kira looked at him. "And if the bulkheads were breached in one of those defenseless parts, internal forcefields would seal the place off, preventing Ops from losing air and other life-support features."

The Bolian grunted. "They had their priorities, all right."

"Hideous though they may have seemed," the Bajoran added. "Particularly if you weren't one of the lucky few picked to work in Ops."

Zar grunted again. "And you learned all this when you took control of the station?" he asked.

"Not me," Kira said. "In the resistance, we studied Cardassian strategy till it was coming out of our ears."

"The resistance?" he echoed.

She could see the mixture of admiration and sympathy in his eyes. But then, she had glimpsed that look before.

"I was part of the Shakaar cell," she told him. "We were better prepared than some of the others."

Zar's eyes narrowed. "That wouldn't be the Shakaar who is first minister of Bajor?" he inquired.

Kira nodded. "One and the same."

He smiled. "Then I'm in distinguished company indeed," he commented. "That is, even more distinguished than I thought."

The irony didn't escape her. There was a time when she hadn't expected to be in any company at all, much less the distinguished kind.

"I'm sorry," the Bolian said quickly, surprising her. "I've brought back some painful memories, haven't I?"

The major realized that she was frowning. A little embarrassed, she laughed and shook her head.

"Don't be sorry," she told him. "It's not your fault they're painful."

Zar seemed to be groping for something to add—something that might ease the discomfort a little. Finally, he could say only: "I've seen some pretty terrible things myself."

Kira looked at him. She wondered what he had experienced that even belonged in the same conversation with the misery she had endured at the hands of the Cardassians.

And then she remembered. The *Saratoga*. Of course.

"Yes," the Bajoran acknowledged. "I guess that *was* pretty terrible."

Zar's eyes took on a faraway look. It was as if he could see the Borg vessel closing in all over again.

Suddenly, Kira found herself wanting to ease *his* pain as he had tried to ease *hers*. She selected her words carefully.

"I've heard about it," she told him, "but I don't really know any of the details. Except that you saved Captain Sisko's life."

The Bolian shrugged. "It was one of those things. You don't think. You just act." He winced. "Jennifer—the captain's wife—was dead already, along with a lot of other people. The ship was a smoking vision of hell. And the Borg were homing in on us, intent on finishing the job they'd started."

"Destroying the *Saratoga*," Kira elaborated.

Zar nodded. "There was damage to the warp core. It was just a question of what got us first—the enemy or our own containment failure. If it had been up to our friend Benjamin, in his numbed and battered state, he would have stayed behind with his wife. He would have tugged and pulled at the charred, twisted wreckage that covered her, until it was too late. And Jake would have wound up an orphan.

"Ultimately," he said, "that was what made my mind up. As you may have noticed, I have a real affection for Jake. Bad enough his mother was a victim. I couldn't see him left without a father as well."

"So you pulled the captain away from her," Kira noted.

"Yes," the Bolian told her, the muscles around his eyes twitching. Yet his tone remained casual, almost conversational. "I turned Jake over to a security officer and gripped my friend with all my strength. And I dragged him back along the ruined corridor, in the direction of the escape pods." He shook his head as he remembered. "Needless to say, he struggled like a crazy person. He tried to free himself with hands already burned and bleeding—denying the fact that his wife was well past his help. And he screamed . . ."

Abruptly, Zar paused. When he picked up the story again, there was a tightness in his voice that hadn't been there before.

"He screamed until his throat was raw," said the Bolian, "pleading for the chance to get Jennifer out of her entrapment. But I wouldn't give him that chance. I fought him every inch of the way to the escape pods.

And with the last of my strength, I shoved him inside."

Bolians were stronger than humans, Kira knew. It was a good thing, too, or Zar might not have accomplished his objective.

Just as she thought that, he turned to her. "Mind you," he added, "the man saved *my* life more times than I can count."

"I understand," she replied. She put her hand on his shoulder. "But that doesn't make what you did any less heroic. Or any less important to those of us who came to know him later on."

Gradually Zar smiled. "You're welcome. And thanks, Major."

"For what?" she asked.

His smile deepened. "For listening."

She shrugged. "Come on," she said, taking his arm. "I'll show you one of the generators—or what's left of it. The Cardassians sabotaged the system before they turned the station over to us."

And without another word, she ushered him into the turbolift.

Odo was sitting at his desk, going over the usual collection of Starfleet security bulletins, when he saw someone approaching his office through its transparent doors. He recognized the man as Aidan Thorn, one of the captain's colleagues on the *Saratoga*.

The shapeshifter frowned. Some of the others on the station had granted Sisko's request that they show his friends around. But Odo was too busy for that. He was a security chief, not a tour guide.

At the man's approach the doors opened. Perhaps if I ignore him, Odo mused, he'll go away.

But it wasn't to be. Thorn walked right up to the changeling's desk as if he owned the place, then stooped over to get its owner's attention.

"Constable?" he said—using a term Odo had come to accept, but not from the mouths of perfect strangers.

Not bothering to stand, he looked up at the human. "Can I help you?" he asked dryly.

"I just thought I'd come by," Thorn said, grinning in his golden brown beard. "After all, we're in the same line of work, us both being security people. And I've never met a—" He shrugged. "You know."

"A changeling," Odo finished for him. "You can say it. It's not a dirty word—at least, not on *this* station."

"I didn't mean to imply that it was," Thorn told him.

He seemed to get the idea he wasn't welcome here. It was an encouraging sign, the shapeshifter thought. Maybe he would take the hint and leave.

"Look," said Thorn, "we seem to have gotten off on the wrong foot. Perhaps I ought to come back some other time."

"Perhaps you should," Odo agreed.

The big man turned to go. Suddenly he stopped and looked back over his shoulder. "By the way," he said, "Tarl Posset says hello." Then he headed for the exit.

Tarl Posset? "Wait a minute," the changeling snapped.

Thorn turned around again. His expression was one big question.

"How do you know Tarl Posset?" Odo asked.

The human shrugged. "Tarl and I go way back. All the way to the academy, I guess, though we didn't really get to be friends till we served on Butera Five. You know, the dilithium processing center?"

"Yes," said Odo, "I've heard him speak of it." He hesitated a moment. Then he indicated an empty chair. "Please. Sit down."

Thorn looked at him. "You sure?"

The shapeshifter nodded. "Positive."

The human sat. "Nice place you've got here. I have to admit, I prefer Federation design to Cardassian. But still, not half-bad."

"It works for me," Odo told him. "That's all I really care about."

"I can see how you would get along well with Tarl," Thorn commented. "He's got the same attitude. Doesn't matter what it looks like, as long as it's functional. As long as it helps him do his job."

"And you?" the shapeshifter inquired.

The big man smiled. "I have some esthetic requirements," he admitted. "Though I'm not as demanding as, say, Joe Simko."

Odo grunted. "You know Joe Simko as well?"

Thorn nodded. "I met *him* back at the Academy, too. Except Joe and I, we hit it off right away. I don't see him as much as I'd like, of course, but we try to keep in touch."

The constable settled back into his seat. "If you know both Tarl and Joe, you must also know how valuable they have been to me. How, when this station was placed under Federation stewardship, I attempted to establish contacts with security personnel on other stations—with little success."

"So I heard," the big man acknowledged. "They were the only two who would give you the time of day—and both of them are now glad of it. From what they told me, they got more information than they gave. At least, in the long run."

Odo harrumphed. "Yes, I suppose they have." He tilted his head. "And where else have you served, Mr. Thorn? Besides the *Gorkon,* of course, and the *Saratoga?* And the dilithium plant on Butera Five?"

"Several places," Thorn replied. He went on to list them. "I've probably skipped around more than I should have, from a career standpoint. But I tend to wear out my commanding officers rather quickly."

"Oh?" said the changeling. "And why is that?"

The human grinned. "I have my little quirks," he conceded. "My own ways of doing things. Not everyone agrees with them, I suppose. But to my way of thinking, the job comes first. If I've kept my ship and my crew from harm, I've done my job. To tell with what anyone thinks of me after that."

"I see," Odo responded.

Perhaps he and Thorn had more in common than

he had first believed. And not just in their choice of friends.

They talked some more, about security technology and Bajor and even Captain Sisko. And the shapeshifter found he didn't mind it in the least. In fact, it was rather pleasant.

"Anyway," said the big man after a while, "I ought to be moving along now. Nice to make your acquaintance, Constable."

The changeling stood. "Likewise, Mr. Thorn."

"Aidan," the human insisted.

"Aidan," said Odo. "And please, er . . . feel free to stop in whenever you like."

Thorn promised he would do that. Then he left.

The changeling grunted. What was that human expression he had heard once? Ah, yes.

You can't judge a book by its cover. He was starting to see the wisdom in it.

When Sisko first arrived on *Deep Space Nine,* he found himself walking the Promenade almost every night, sometimes far into the morning. He would stare out the large, majestic observation ports at the stars, and try helplessly to imagine what a man like him might do in a place like this.

There was no one else around at that time of night. Not even Odo—at least, as far as the captain knew. And Sisko had been glad of it. After all, he could find the answers to his questions only in himself.

In time, of course, the answers came. He established an equilibrium here, a sense of purpose. A feeling that this station, with all its difficulties and all its dangers, was nonetheless his home.

And that was the day he stopped haunting the Promenade.

Until now, he thought, as he strolled along the upper level, gazing at the cold, distant stars. But then, it came as no surprise to him that he couldn't sleep this night.

Tomorrow, he and his former comrades would take off for the fleet yards orbiting Mars. Once again, he would be forced to confront his past. And though he had been glad to see Zar and the others, he still wasn't certain how he would react to the sight of a brand-new *Saratoga*.

"Captain Sisko?"

He turned at the sound of his name, spoken by a feminine voice. He saw, at the far end of the walkway, the slender figure of Counselor Barnes.

The woman smiled as she approached. It wasn't a bad smile, either. Much more appealing than the poor, perfunctory thing he had seen her exhibit earlier, on her arrival.

"What brings you out here at this hour of the night?" he inquired.

Not that he didn't already know the answer. He was just doing his best to be polite.

Barnes shrugged. "I felt the urge to roam. To be less . . . I don't know. Cooped up, I suppose." She paused. "And you?"

"The same," he said, "more or less."

Her smile faded a little. "You look like you want to be alone right now. Maybe I should make myself scarce." She turned to go.

"No," he replied, without even thinking about it. It surprised him that he had said the word.

The counselor turned to look back at him. "Are you sure?" she asked. "I don't want to intrude."

Sisko shook his head. "You're not. Really."

Barnes peered into his eyes for confirmation. "All right," she said at last. "As long as you're certain."

As he resumed his walk, she joined him. For a time, they strolled in silence, neither of them speaking. And yet, the captain didn't feel the least bit uncomfortable about the silence.

He began to understand why Kyprios valued the counselor's services so much. Barnes exuded a kind of calm that he hadn't noticed in her before. She made one feel at ease—not only with her, but with oneself.

"The stars are lovely here," she commented.

He nodded. "Yes, they are. But then, as I recall, they're pretty lovely wherever you go."

She seemed to think about that for a moment. "I guess they are," she responded, "when you stop to look at them. But on a ship, you seldom do. You're always on your way somewhere."

Sisko saw what she meant. "All you're looking at are trails of light. Not the stars themselves, really, but a warp-speed representation of them."

"Exactly," said the counselor. "When our ancestors looked up at the heavens, they didn't see light trails, or warp-speed representations. They saw perfect little gems."

He had to admit, he hadn't thought of it that way. He said so.

"Neither had I," Barnes admitted. She grinned at the realization. "At least until now."

He grinned, too. He couldn't help it. There was something contagious about the woman's demeanor.

"So," the counselor resumed finally, "what do you see in these stars? What kind of future do they hold for Benjamin Sisko?"

He looked at her. "What are my aspirations, you mean?" He drew a breath, then let it out. "I don't think I've thought that far ahead, really. For the time being, of course, there's plenty to be done here. I don't see myself going anywhere else for a good long time." He paused. "And you?"

Barnes laughed, as if he had touched on some secret joke. "If you ask Captain Kyprios, he'll tell you that I'm not going anywhere—other than where the *Endeavor* takes me."

"But you're not so sure about that," Sisko observed.

"Not at all," she confirmed. "I just don't feel as if I've found my place yet in the scheme of things."

"Oh?" he replied.

"Don't get me wrong," the counselor told him. "Serving on the *Endeavor* has been a terrific experience and all, and I've learned a lot from Captain Kyprios. But it's not what I want to do with the rest of my life."

As she looked at him, having so easily opened herself up to a perfect stranger, the captain couldn't help but admire her courage. And that wasn't all he found himself admiring.

There was a light in her eyes he hadn't noticed before. It wasn't just a reflection of the starlight through the observation port, either. It was a light from within.

Sisko found himself unexpectedly intrigued by her. He wasn't sure in what way, though—as a friend or a lover.

What's more, he wasn't going to allow himself to find out. He already had a good thing going with Kasidy Yates, and he wasn't the type of man to flit from one relationship to another.

Suddenly, a familiar voice rang out along the Promenade: "Dad?"

The captain turned and saw his son ascending a stairway from the lower level. His first reaction was a fatherly one—to wonder what Jake was still doing up at this hour.

"I know," the boy told him, as he stopped at the top of the stairs. "It's past my bedtime." He glanced at Counselor Barnes. "And believe me, I wouldn't be out here, if it wasn't for Admiral Pardee."

Sisko felt the color drain from his face. "Admiral Pardee," he repeated numbly. He sighed.

The intelligence report on Dominion trade routes in the Gamma Quadrant. In all the excitement over seeing his old friends, he had forgotten all about it—and he was supposed to have filed it two days ago.

"The admiral seemed pretty insistent," Jake reported. "He wanted to speak to you directly, but I told him you were in a part of the station where you couldn't be reached."

Sisko nodded appreciatively. "Thanks, Jake-o."

"Is something wrong?" asked Barnes.

"Nothing earthshaking," the captain explained. "Just a bureaucratic detail I've managed to put aside much too long. And unfortunately, it can't wait until I get back from Utopia Planitia."

He shrugged, by way of apology. It seemed their stroll had come to a rather abrupt end.

"That's all right," the counselor assured him. "I was starting to feel a little worn out anyway, and we do have a long trip ahead of us. Good night, Captain Sisko."

Sisko inclined his head. "Good night, Counselor Barnes."

He watched her for a moment as she turned around and walked back the way she came. Then he frowned and descended the stairs with his son.

"I didn't interrupt anything, did I?" asked the boy.

The captain looked at him. "I have no romantic designs on the counselor, if that's what you mean. She's strictly a colleague."

Jake smiled. "Whatever you say, Dad."

Sisko wasn't sure, but he thought he heard a note of skepticism in his son's voice. "What do you mean, whatever I say?"

His son shrugged. "Nothing, Dad. Really."

The captain was about to press the issue, then thought better of it. If there had been something more than friendship in the way he looked at Barnes, he didn't want to know about it.

Hell, life was complicated enough. The last thing he needed was to be seeing *two* women.

CHAPTER
7

Kira stood in Ops and watched Sisko enter the lift, followed closely by O'Brien and Dax. After they were all inside, the captain turned to her.

"Have a good time," she told him.

Sisko gave her a look that told her he would try, though he had his doubts. Then he tapped the padd in the lift that gave it its marching orders. A moment later, the trio began to descend to the docking level.

The last thing Kira saw of them was Dax's smile— the Trill's way of assuring her friend that she would take care of their commanding officer. But then, the Bajoran had no doubt of that.

Once they were no longer in sight, Kira turned around and assessed her Ops contingent. While none of the senior staff was on hand except her, they were all veterans. She didn't expect any problems from them.

Hell, she didn't expect any problems at all. But it didn't hurt to be prepared, so she had her people run a level one diagnostic of all major systems. Just in case.

They had barely finished when one of them—a Bajoran—raised her head. "The *Defiant* is ready to depart," she reported.

"Retract docking clamps," Kira responded.

"Clamps retracted," the woman told her.

"Release tractor lock," Kira instructed.

"Tractors released," came the reply.

Abruptly the Cardassian monitor at the front of the Ops facility came alive with Sisko's image. The captain looked serious—much *too* serious. This was just a courtesy run, not a suicide mission.

Sisko frowned. "The station is all yours, Major."

Kira smiled. "Only until you get back, sir."

The captain's frown deepened. Without another word, he ended the transmission. His face was instantly replaced by the sight of the *Defiant* as it backed off from its docking pylon and then, applying thrusters, veered away from the station.

The Bajoran shook her head. In a way, she was glad that Sisko had seen fit to leave her behind. Things were liable to be much more cheerful around here, she suspected, than alongside the captain.

Truth to tell, Sisko could have gotten along without Dax and O'Brien, too. Several of his former comrades were accomplished pilots, after all. And with Graal aboard, there would have been no shortage of technical smarts.

But the captain had insisted on bringing personnel who were familiar with the *Defiant's* idiosyncrasies. Hence, the presence of Dax and O'Brien. And though Kira certainly fit that bill as well as the other two, she was also the first officer—and therefore the person best qualified to run the station in Sisko's absence.

As she watched the *Defiant* shift to impulse power and recede into the field of stars, the major was reminded of another departure in which she had an abiding interest. Unless she was mistaken, Quark's ship was scheduled to be getting under way pretty soon.

Knowing the Ferengi as she did, she resolved to check with him about it. With so much at stake for her friends in Karvis, she didn't want to have to worry about any last-minute mishaps.

For the next fifteen minutes or so she remained at her post, making sure there was nothing that required her attention. Then she headed for Quark's.

She had barely reached the Promenade when she ran into Rom. *Literally.*

The Ferengi looked up at her, eyes wide with anxiety, hands clenched into tight little fists. He looked as if someone had stolen his last bar of gold-pressed latinum.

"Major," cried Rom, "I'm so glad to see you. Something has happened—something terrible."

Kira sighed. "What's the matter, Rom? Is there a holosuite on the blink? Or maybe you've run out of those salty little beer nuts Morn's so partial to?"

"No," moaned the Ferengi. "It's even worse than that. My *brother* has fallen into a . . . a coma or something."

Suddenly the Bajoran felt as if someone had phaser-blasted her in the stomach. She looked at Rom.

"I want you to repeat that," Kira said, trying to keep her emotions in check. "And I want you to repeat it slowly."

"It's my brother," Rom whined. "He . . . he fainted, just as he was getting ready to leave for his rendezvous with Fel Jangor. And I can't revive him." The Ferengi wrung his hands. "You've got to do something, Major."

Kira cursed under her breath. It sounded bad. Tapping her communicator, she looked up instinctively at the station's intercom system.

"Kira to Dr. Bashir."

The doctor took only a moment to respond. "Yes, Major. What can I do for you?"

"It's Quark," the Ferengi interjected, unable to contain himself. "He's fallen into some kind of coma."

"Rom may be jumping to conclusions," the major commented. "But there *does* seem to be something wrong. I'll meet you in Quark's quarters."

"Acknowledged," said Bashir.

As Kira headed in that direction, Quark's brother

ran along beside her, trying desperately to match her longer strides. "Do you think there'll be any permanent damage?" he asked.

The Bajoran grunted. "Only if he's faking," she decided.

It didn't take them long to reach the Ferengi's quarters. Or, with Rom's participation, to bypass Quark's multitudinous security systems.

"Quark's always saying how you can't trust anyone these days," Rom noted, as the doors opened on his brother's anteroom. "In fact, according to him, you never *could.*"

"Where is he?" asked Kira, ignoring the Ferengi philosophy.

"This way," said Rom, scurrying past her toward the back room that apparently served as Quark's bedchamber.

Following the Ferengi, the major caught sight of a couple of boots strewn on the section of floor framed in the open doorway. It wasn't until Kira got closer that she realized Quark's feet were still in them. He was stretched out as if some irate customer had leveled him.

No—there was a difference. If he'd been knocked out, he wouldn't have had those faint purple splotches all over his face.

Turning to her, Rom gasped. "Those marks," he breathed. "They weren't there before, Major."

Kneeling beside the unconscious Ferengi, Kira loosened his brocaded collar. The skin of Quark's face felt cold and clammy to the touch—though as she recalled, it pretty much always felt that way. In any case, he still had a nice strong pulse.

Peering over her shoulder, Rom grunted. "You know," he said, "if I didn't know better, I'd say those were *gruw'r* spots."

The major looked back over her shoulder at him. *"Gruw'r* spots?" she echoed. "And what in the name of the Prophets are *those?"*

"It's very simple, really," Bashir explained. *"Gruw'r* spots are what you get when you contract *gruw'r*—a childhood disease rather common among the Ferengi, much as mumps or chicken pox used to be common on Earth."

He was examining Quark in the infirmary, having brought the unconscious Ferengi here with the help of Kira, Rom, and a couple of station personnel. It hadn't taken him long to run a few tests—or to figure out what was wrong.

"And is that what Quark's got?" Kira inquired. "This . . . *gruw'r?"*

Casting a glance over his shoulder at his patient, the doctor nodded. "Yes. Of course, the vast majority of Ferengi seem to catch it before the age of nine, and then never again. Quark must have been an exception."

"That's right," Rom confirmed, plumbing his memory. "I got *gruw'r* when I was six. But Quark never did, for some reason."

"Some people just don't," Bashir told him. "They have a natural immunity. But over the years, that immunity tends to fade. That's what happened to our friend here, apparently. His immunity faded."

Quark's brother grunted. "So when he came in contact with someone carrying the disease . . ."

"He came down with it in an Andorian minute," the doctor said, finishing the thought for him. "What's more, the bug could've been carried by anybody, not just a Ferengi." He smiled sympathetically at Rom. "And the tests show it wasn't you. So Quark will have a hard time finding someone to blame when he wakes up."

"That's a relief," Rom replied earnestly.

"So how fast can you cure him?" asked Kira, clearly more interested in that detail than any other.

She'd already confided in Bashir about the mission Quark was involved in, and what it meant to Bajor. With that in mind, he knew she wasn't going to like what he had to tell her.

"I can't," he said simply.

"You've got to," the major insisted.

The doctor shook his head. "In a child, this is not a dangerous disease. But when it affects an adult, it *can* be dangerous. It's also very difficult to treat. I'm afraid I can't allow the patient to leave the infirmary, even when he regains consciousness."

Kira held her hands out to him. "There's got to be a way," she began. "Something to suppress the symptoms . . ."

"No," he told her, standing firm. "There *is* no way. If I let Quark go, he won't be in any shape to do what you need him to. And on top of that, he could die."

That was a difficult argument to knock down. The major's disappointment was evident in her face, her hands, her entire body.

After all, Kira had been on the verge of solving her friend's problem—on the verge of saving a lot of people from a lot of hardship. And now, her solution was crumbling before her eyes.

Bashir's heart went out to her. However, as was sometimes the case in the medical profession, there was nothing he could do.

"I see," the major responded numbly.

Rom tugged on Kira's sleeve. "Wait a minute," he declared. "Maybe we can still do what you wanted us to."

The Bajoran frowned. "Come on, Rom. You heard Dr. Bashir. Quark can't be moved from this place."

The Ferengi looked up at her. "I know that. But Quark isn't the only one who knows how to negotiate a deal."

Kira's eyes narrowed. "What are you saying?"

Rom heaved an impatient sigh. "I'm saying that I'm a Ferengi, too. I studied the Rules of Acquisition just as Quark did. And though I may not be as good as my brother, I've made a few transactions in my day."

The major put a hand on the Ferengi's shoulder, a token of her gratitude. "Nice try," she said. "But Jangor won't negotiate with you. You're not the one who saved his life, remember? It's Quark he has a soft spot for."

Rom started to protest—then caught himself. His head dropped as if he were a puppet and someone had cut his strings. "I guess you're right," he conceded. "Jangor will only trust Quark, and Quark's not—"

Abruptly the Ferengi's head snapped up. There was a light in his eyes that would normally have reflected an opportunity to acquire large quantities of latinum—though Bashir had a feeling that, this time at least, it signified something else.

"Hang on," Rom told them. "Maybe Quark *can* be there."

The doctor gave the Ferengi his full attention. This, he had to hear.

It never took Odo long to find out anything that took place on the station. In fact, he prided himself on that ability.

So when Quark was taken to Dr. Bashir's infirmary, the constable got wind of it rather quickly. And just as quickly, he made his way in that direction.

Despite appearances to the contrary that he'd worked rather hard to construct, he felt a certain kinship with the Ferengi. After all, they were both square pegs in round holes around here.

Quark, because his values differed so much from those of the station's other residents. And Odo, because . . . well, because he was a shapeshifter, whose people were perhaps the greatest threat to the

Federation in its long history. Those were *two* big reasons right there.

What's more, the Ferengi was the only one on *Deep Space Nine* who shared Odo's interest in criminology. Of course, Quark was looking at it from the side of the criminal, but he was nonetheless interested. Nor was it unusual for a lawman and his prey to find they had more in common with each other than they did with the community at large.

The constable was just mulling over that irony when he saw Kira and Rom coming toward him, from the other end of the corridor. What's more, they were discussing something in rather animated tones.

Apparently, Odo mused, Quark wasn't that badly off. Otherwise, the major and her companion would have been a lot more solemn.

"It won't work," said Kira, making a gesture of dismissal with her hand. "Besides, Odo will never do it."

Stopping squarely in their path, the shapeshifter cleared his throat. "What won't I do?" he asked.

The major looked up at him. Rom, too.

Kira smiled. "Nothing," she assured him.

"How do you know?" Odo pressed.

"I know," said the major.

"I think you're wrong," the Ferengi maintained.

The constable sighed. "Wrong about what?"

Kira and Rom looked at each other. Finally it was the Ferengi who spoke.

"I'm saying you'll help the major out of a mess," Rom told him. "And she says you'll refuse."

Kira shook her head. "It's not that simple, Odo."

"Yes, it is," the Ferengi insisted. He cast a sidelong glance at the constable. "Either he'll help or he won't."

Odo straightened. He gazed at Kira, whom he held in more than amiable esteem. In point of fact, he was in love with her, though he would never have dared to come out and say so.

"I'm afraid," he said, "Rom is right in this instance. If I can help, all you have to do is say the word."

The major looked at him, obviously a bit uncomfortable with the carte blanche he'd just handed her. "You're sure?" she prodded.

"I'm sure," he confirmed.

Kira looked as if she'd have liked to say more. However, the Ferengi interrupted her.

"It's a deal," he announced, grasping Odo's hand and shaking it. "And believe me, you won't regret it."

"Oh, yes, he will," the major replied.

And to the constable's mounting chagrin, she told him just what he'd gotten himself into.

CHAPTER
8

O'BRIEN WAS DEEP into his shift at the *Defiant*'s helm when he got the feeling there was someone standing in back of him. Old instincts taking over, he whirled, ready for anything.

But it wasn't an invader. At least, not in the strictest sense. It was Graal, her round black eyes as inscrutable as ever.

At the far end of the bridge, Dax was running some diagnostic routines on her science console. If she had noticed Graal's entrance, she didn't give any sign of it.

Frowning, the chief tried to tell himself the Craynid hadn't spooked him on purpose. She was just naturally quiet in the way she moved about.

"Yes?" he prompted.

For a moment or two, there was silence. It seemed

to O'Brien that Graal was thinking about something—and as usual, taking her time.

"Chief?" she rasped finally.

He sighed. "Yes, Commander?" He did his best to keep the impatience out of his voice.

Fortunately there weren't any big, heavy things for O'Brien to lug about on the *Defiant*. His back was still sore from all the lifting and twisting and pulling he had done back on the station.

"I believe you have missed an opportunity," the Craynid remarked.

He grunted. "An opportunity?"

"Yes," she hissed. "To improve the efficiency of this vessel."

The chief could taste the bile rising in his throat. "Really," he responded. "Well, with all due respect, Commander, I'd be surprised if that were the case, seeing as how I've been over the *Defiant* with a fine-tooth comb. In fact, make that several fine-tooth combs."

And he had, too. It was one thing to criticize the way he outfitted *Deep Space Nine,* considering all the problems he had inherited from the Cardassians. But he knew starship engineering as well as anyone in the fleet, and the *Defiant*'s best of all.

"Nonetheless," Graal insisted, "there is room for improvement."

O'Brien wanted to tell her where to get off. But of course, he couldn't. She outranked him. And even if rank weren't a factor, the Craynid was a friend of Captain Sisko.

So he bit his tongue and maintained his composure. He even attempted a smile, though he didn't imagine it worked out very well.

"Well," the chief replied, "I'd be glad to explore this with you further, as soon as my shift is over."

Graal seemed to ponder his response. Then she said, "That will be satisfactory." And without any further ceremony, she moved off in the direction of the turbolift.

O'Brien turned back to his controls and chewed the inside of his cheek. There had been times in his life when he couldn't wait for his shift to end.

This wasn't one of them.

Odo gasped. "You want me to *what?*"

Kira looked at him sympathetically. "I knew you weren't going to like the idea. But it really would be a great help to the people of Karvis."

"And besides," Rom pointed out from under his nose, "we made a deal."

The constable backed him off with a glare. "That was before I knew what you were suggesting," he argued.

"A deal is a deal," the Ferengi insisted.

Odo turned to the major again, seeking understanding. "But the thought of assuming Quark's form"—He shuddered inwardly.—"is anathema to me. And the idea of participating in Ferengi-style *negotiation . . ."*

"I know," said Kira. "It'd send shivers up *my* spine as well."

Technically speaking, of course, the shapeshifter didn't have a spine. Or for that matter, a musculature with which to shiver. But he understood all too well what his friend was talking about.

"What's more," he went on, "I wouldn't be very good at what you're asking of me. I'd be a terrible negotiator. And you know I can't create precise likenesses—not of Quark or anyone else."

He wasn't lying, either. If he'd been able to assume a perfect humanoid appearance, he'd have done so a long time ago—instead of walking around with vague, half-formed features.

"That's where *I* come in," Rom interjected, stepping between Odo and his friend. He looked up at the shapeshifter. "I'll guide you through the negotiation step by step. And as for creating a precise likeness . . ." He shrugged. "Don't give it a second thought. Jangor is half-blind. If you look even a little bit like Quark, he won't suspect a thing."

Odo frowned at the Ferengi. *"You* look a little like Quark *already*. Why don't you do this yourself?"

"Because Quark already agreed to bring me," Rom argued. "If I show up alone, pretending to be Quark, he'll know something is wrong."

The constable was starting to feel cornered. It wasn't a pleasant experience. And if it weren't Kira who was asking this of him, he would never even have considered such a degrading notion.

"Listen," said the Bajoran, seeming to read his thoughts. She looked sympathetic. "If it weren't such an important cause, I wouldn't ask. But Karvis really *needs* those power coils."

Odo didn't have a chance. When Kira looked at him that way, he melted. Not literally, of course, but pretty close to it.

He made a sound of defeat mixed with disgust. "All right," he agreed finally. "I'll give it a try—though I'm still not convinced it'll work."

More likely, the changeling told himself, the result would be not only failure but humiliation for all parties concerned. And he would be the most humiliated one of all.

Dax looked up from her science console on the bridge of the *Defiant*. For the second time in the last hour, she watched Commander Graal approach Chief O'Brien. And for the second time in the last hour, she saw the chief whirl as if some enemy were trying to sneak up on him.

"Oh," said O'Brien. "It's you again . . . sir."

Graal had no outward reaction to the remark. "I believe your shift is over," she observed.

As Dax watched the chief check the chronometer in his control panel, she glanced at her own. Sure enough, O'Brien's tour was coming to a close.

As if to punctuate the Craynid's comment, the turbolift doors opened and Lieutenant Thorn emerged. He headed for the pilot's chair with a clear and undisguised gusto for the task ahead of him.

The chief sighed. "I suppose you're right," he told Graal.

With a reluctance that looked almost painful from Dax's vantage point, O'Brien got up from his post and gave way to Thorn. It seemed to her that Thorn glanced sympathetically at his fellow human before seating himself—and that O'Brien noted the gesture.

Then, as the chief followed the Craynid toward the lift, Thorn acclimated himself to the helm controls. It didn't take him more than a minute to get comfortable, and even to make a few small adjustments.

Dax smiled at the man's enthusiasm, and also at his skill. From what she could see on her monitors, Thorn's adjustments had been good ones.

"I can see you've done this before," Dax remarked.

Thorn turned to her, his broad face suddenly split by a big, disarming smile. It would be difficult to dislike this man, she imagined.

"Once or twice," he joked, his blue eyes gleaming merrily. "You see, before I was a security officer, I was one of the best damned pilots to come out of the Academy."

The Trill grunted. "Modest, aren't we?"

"It's no brag," the man assured her. "You can ask any flight instructor I ever had. In fact, my very first day on the *Victory,* I was assigned to the conn station."

That piqued Dax's interest. "The *Victory,* you say? I knew someone once who served on the *Victory.* A Vulcan named Simora."

Thorn's smile faded just a bit. "You knew Simora, did you?"

The Trill nodded. "We met when she came through

115

here with the *Wellington*. Smart lady. Sort of quiet. And one hell of a cook. By the time she left, I was making *plomeek* soup with the best of them."

The security officer shrugged. "You got along with Simora better than I did, apparently. I think I was a bit too—oh, I don't know—*blustery* for her tastes, a bit too rambunctious. But then, she wasn't very fond of humans in general, it seemed to me."

Dax looked at him thoughtfully. After a moment, she nodded. "Yup," she said. "That's Simora, all right."

And without further comment, she turned her attention back to her console. But in truth, her attention was focused elsewhere.

As O'Brien followed the Craynid out of the lift, he was amazed once more by her slow and almost painful-looking approach to locomotion. It occurred to him that evolution was more efficient on some planets than others.

But then, comparative biology was more Julian's field than his own. O'Brien was an engineer. And Graal had at least hinted there was a need for a man of his talents down here on the life-support deck, or he wouldn't have come in the first place.

"Can you tell me a bit more about the problem?" he asked her.

She didn't turn to look at him. She just stared at the corridor up ahead. Obviously, she was pretty intent on something, though the human still wasn't sure what.

"Not even a clue?" he prodded.

"You will see soon enough," she whistled.

Soon enough, he echoed inwardly. Well, I can tell you, that makes me feel a whole lot better. Nothing I look forward to more, after a full tour of duty on the bridge, than following some tight-mouthed Craynid who-knows-where for who-knows-what.

Abruptly his companion stopped and looked around. After a moment, she seemed to find what she was looking for. With something like a sigh, she approached the local node for the inertial damper system.

It was housed in a perfectly square box mounted onto the bulkhead. To the untrained eye, it probably looked like all the other perfectly square boxes up and down the corridor. That is, until that untrained eye got close enough to read the graphic on the thing.

"This," hissed the former chief engineer of the *Saratoga.*

O'Brien looked at her. "There's something wrong with the damper node? Some kind of malfunction?"

Graal shook her oversize head from side to side. No doubt, she'd picked up the gesture from working with humans for so long.

"Something's wrong," she confirmed. "But it's not a malfunction." The Craynid leaned closer to him. "Sabotage," she whispered.

O'Brien hadn't expected her to say that. For a moment, he thought she was mistaken. Then he remembered that business with the circuitry back on *Deep Space Nine.*

Frowning, he removed the housing from the node and set it down on the floor. What he saw inside was a series of knoblike projections, permeated with tiny emitters and connected by power cables.

They seemed functional and untouched. But just to be certain, O'Brien took out his tricorder and ran it over the whole affair. Then he eyed the device's tiny readout—and saw there was something wrong indeed.

Muttering a curse beneath his breath, he looked up at Graal. "You're right," he blurted. "Someone's tampered with this thing. If we were to accelerate suddenly, this section of the ship would be structurally at risk. An entire piece of the hull could collapse."

The Craynid didn't remark on his observation directly. "It will take work to correct," was her only response.

He held up the tricorder so she could see the readout. "A good deal of it," he agreed.

But that was far from the most disturbing aspect of their discovery. Shaking his head, O'Brien looked at the node in a new light.

Who on this ship would want to tamper with the inertial dampers? And more important . . . for what purpose?

Odo hooked a forefinger around his stiff brocaded collar and tugged—to no avail. The damned thing was just as uncomfortable and unyielding as before.

Of course, the rest of his surroundings were quite comfortable—almost *too* comfortable. Ostentatious, one might say. But then, this was a hired spacecraft. The more luxurious the environment, the more its grasping captain could charge for it.

Glancing to his right, the changeling again considered the mirrorlike surface that decorated the bulkhead beside him. In it, he could see his reflection. Or rather, to his chagrin, *Quark's* reflection.

"What's the matter?" asked Rom, who was returning from the next cabin with a platter of replicated delicacies.

Odo frowned as he regarded the mirror. "It's not quite right," he observed. "The frontal lobes aren't prominent enough."

"They're fine," the Ferengi told him.

"No, they're not," the constable insisted.

He willed them to grow a bit. Before his eyes, they complied.

"Stop that," said Rom, putting his platter on a small table.

The changeling looked at him. "Look, it's bad enough I have to go through with this incredibly stupid charade. At least allow me the opportunity to do it right."

"Doing it right," the Ferengi argued, "will be more a matter of behavior than appearance. Now, I assume you've memorized everything?"

Odo rolled his eyes disparagingly. "You mean your Rules of Acquisition? Yes, I've memorized them—as much as it pained me to do so."

"Good," said Rom, sitting down beside the likeness of his brother. "Then recite Rule Sixteen for me."

The constable turned on him. "What?"

"You heard me," the Ferengi replied. "If you can't recite the Rules of Acquisition as the occasion demands, you'll never get Jangor to believe you're my brother."

Odo cursed out loud—though it wasn't difficult to see the sense in Rom's advice. "Very well, then. Rule Sixteen. *A deal is a deal until a better one comes along.*"

The Ferengi grinned. "Very good, Constable. Very good indeed. And Rule One hundred thirty-nine?"

The changeling sighed. *"Wives serve, brothers inherit."*

Quark's brother rubbed his hands together eagerly. "Yes, perfect. That's one of my favorites."

"I'm not surprised," Odo commented.

"Rule Fifty-nine?" Rom prodded.

"Free advice is seldom cheap," the constable responded.

"Forty-eight?"

"The bigger the smile, the sharper the knife."

"Thirty-three?"

"It never hurts to suck up to the boss," Odo answered, at the end of his rope. "And then there's Rule Six, of course. You know that one, don't you? *Never allow family to stand in the way of opportunity.*"

The Ferengi's smile faded quickly. "I never saw the wisdom in that one myself, I must admit. But it's good to have it at your disposal." He paused. "What about our hand signals?"

"Don't worry," said the shapeshifter. "I've memorized those as well. Palms up, I'm to agree with Jangor. Palms down, I'm to disagree. And—"

Abruptly the door to their cabin opened again. Their pilot, an Yridian, walked in unannounced.

"I hope you're enjoying the trip," he said, though it was clear he didn't give a damn one way or the other.

Odo cleared his throat. "You'd better hope so," he said, doing his best impression of Quark. "I'm not in the habit of paying for top accommodations and not receiving them."

Of course, the Yridian didn't know Quark very well, having spoken to him only once or twice, so he wasn't much of a critic. But to the changeling's relief, he seemed fooled.

"Whatever you say, Ferengi. If you like, you can contact your friend now. We're in communications range of his vessel."

"Excellent," Odo replied. "But I think I can wait—"

"What my brother means," said Rom, "was he'd be delighted to speak with Fel Jangor."

The Yridian looked from one to the other of them. "What's it to be?" he asked.

Taking the hint, the shapeshifter sighed deeply. "Go ahead and contact the fellow," he confirmed.

Their pilot nodded, then left them to themselves. Reluctantly Odo stood and turned toward the elaborately decorated pentagonal viewscreen that graced one of the bulkheads.

A moment later, he saw a thickset, almost globular-looking figure appear on the screen. His pale, mottled skin and blunted features told the changeling this was a Retizian. And the length of the black quills that protruded from the fellow's chins, denoting advanced old age, told him this was very likely Fel Jangor.

As Rom came to stand beside his "brother," the Retizian squinted at the two of them. Apparently his eyesight was every bit as bad as the Ferengi had indicated.

"Fel Jangor," said Rom, in his most ingratiating—and therefore annoying—tone. "It's so good to see you again."

The Retizian nodded. "Is that you, Quark? You don't sound like yourself."

Odo drew himself up to his full, albeit diminutive, height. It was now or never, he told himself.

"No, Fel Jangor. That's my brother, Rom." The constable affected a smile. *"I'm* Quark, over here." He waved, for good measure.

The Retizian looked him up and down for what seemed like an eternity. Odo began to wonder if he'd missed something important. But how could that be? If Rom hadn't noticed anything, how could Jangor?

Then, much to his relief, the Retizian smiled back. "Yes, of course," he replied. "My old friend Quark. It seems my sight gets worse and worse every cycle. That's not good, when you're a wanted man."

The changeling shrugged, as if that didn't matter to him. "We're *all* wanted *somewhere,* aren't we?"

Jangor laughed—a sound more like barking than the kind of laughter Odo was used to. "You always did have a way with words," the Retizian said. "But . . ." He squinted again.

"Yes?" the shapeshifter responded.

"Now that I think about it, you don't look so well," Jangor observed. "You're not ill, are you?"

In fact, he *felt* ill. The whole idea of impersonating Quark made him more than a little queasy. But of course, he couldn't say that.

"I've caught some sort of virus," Odo explained. "Nothing serious, mind you. It's good of you to notice."

"A good businessman can't help but notice," said the Retizian.

"How true," the changeling returned. "And you are a good businessman. You know," he continued, changing the subject, "I'm looking forward to this negotiation. In fact, it may be just the cure I need."

Jangor grunted. "I hope so, old friend. I'll make arrangements to have you beamed aboard my vessel."

"Excellent," Odo told him.

A moment later, the viewscreen went blank. The constable turned to Rom.

"How did I do?" he asked.

The Ferengi nodded. "You did well—better than I expected, in fact. I don't think Jangor suspects a thing."

So far so good, thought Odo. He tugged again at his collar. Now if I can just loosen this blasted thing . . .

CHAPTER 9

As Sisko entered the turbolift on his way to the bridge, he saw that Lopez was already inside. The science officer smiled.

"It's about time you showed up, sir."

Entering the lift, the captain cocked an eyebrow. "Insubordination, Mr. Lopez?"

"Perish the thought," his old colleague replied. "Bridge," he commanded. "And don't spare the horses."

The doors closed. In a matter of moments, they opened again—this time on their destination. Lopez indicated with a sweep of his arm that Sisko should exit first.

"Rank has its privileges," he remarked.

"I see you've learned *something* since the *Saratoga*," the captain quipped, emerging onto the bridge.

"Ouch," said Lopez, following him out.

As Sisko headed for his captain's chair, the science officer made his way to the helm position. Dax, who had manned that post for the last few hours, turned at Lopez's approach. So did Thorn.

"I hope your watch is as pleasant as mine was," the big man told his friend.

Lopez looked at the Trill as he answered. "How can it be?" he remarked pointedly.

Smiling at the compliment, Dax got up to give the science officer her seat. But before she could be on her way, Lopez caught her gently by the hand.

"It seems we're like two ships passing in the dark of space," he observed, "coming close but never quite meeting."

Dax looked impressed. "I like the metaphor," she admitted.

"I hoped you would," he told her earnestly.

"Of course," she went on cordially, "some ships never *do* meet. They just keep on passing each other."

Withdrawing her hand, she left him openmouthed. A moment later, she entered the turbolift.

As the doors closed, the captain used his hand to cover the lower half of his face, so Lopez couldn't see him chuckling. Thorn, on the other hand, didn't bother to conceal anything. He laughed out loud, until the bridge was ringing with it.

"Go ahead and laugh," declared the science officer.

"All right," said the big man, "I will." And he laughed some more.

The captain couldn't help but enjoy Lopez's discomfort. "I'll bet it's been a long time since anyone turned you down, Esteban. And not once but twice, as I understand it."

Lopez shrugged. "It's a long trip, sir. Anything can happen."

Sisko smiled. "I admire your attitude. But you'll find Lieutenant Dax isn't the sort to—"

Before he could complete the sentence, he felt himself catapulted out of his seat. For the fraction of a second that he was hurtling forward, he wondered what had happened—what had gone wrong.

Then he hit the hard surface of the deck, slid, and slammed with bone-jarring force into the base of one of the bridge consoles. It left him stunned, with the metallic taste of blood in his mouth.

For a moment the bridge went dark, the only light that of a geysering shower of sparks from one of the control consoles. Then, with a flicker or two, the illumination returned.

Struggling mightily to clear his head, the captain looked up and saw his friends had been tossed about as well. Fortunately neither of them had been knocked unconscious.

"What the hell was *that?*" he demanded, gathering his feet beneath him. As he made his way back to the captain's chair on legs too wobbly for his liking, he noticed the viewscreen had gone black.

"I wish I knew," replied Lopez, dragging himself back up to a standing position, despite some nasty-looking bruises on the side of his face. He began tapping at the control padds on the nearest console, trying to make sense of things.

"It felt like we *hit* something," said Thorn, who had by then made his way to the helm controls.

Sisko looked to the intercom grid concealed in the ceiling. "Dr. Laffer, I want a casualty report."

Silence.

"Dr. Laffer?" the captain repeated.

Again, no answer.

He muttered a curse. "Zar?"

"Here, sir," the Bolian replied.

"Put together a casualty report, Lieutenant. And find Dr. Laffer. She's not answering my call."

"Aye, sir," said Zar.

Sisko turned to the console on his right and requested a damage report with a few quick touches. The response was instantaneous.

The majority of ship's systems had been jolted to one degree or another. Some of the sensors had been damaged, which explained the lack of an image on the viewscreen. And the *Defiant*'s cloaking capabilities had been lost, at least for the time being.

However, propulsion was clearly in the worst shape of all. Both impulse and warp engines were off-line, and would require some attention before they could be of any use.

Also, the escape pods had been wrecked rather thoroughly. The captain shook his head, wondering how that could be. After all, the escape pods had been thoroughly secured prior to departure from *Deep Space Nine*.

He called up some further information, which unraveled the mystery. Apparently the inertial dampers in that section of the *Defiant* weren't working. So when the impact came, there was nothing to stop the pods from getting banged around.

But it was highly unusual for a set of dampers to conk out like that. They were usually among the *last* pieces of equipment to go off-line. Sisko wished he had more time to contemplate the situation, to try to puzzle it out. However, he had more immediate concerns.

Turning to Lopez and Thorn, he was about to ask them if they had figured out the cause of the impact. But before he could get a word out, Zar's voice rang out across the bridge.

"Zar to Sisko. Come in, Captain."

"Sisko here. What's happening, Lieutenant?"

"We have Dr. Laffer, sir. She's unconscious, the result of a head injury."

"How bad is she?" asked the captain.

"We don't know yet," the Bolian replied, his voice taut. "Dax and I have stabilized her, but we're not physicians. It's going to take a while to develop a prognosis, I'm afraid."

Sisko shook his head. It was a terrible irony. If anyone else but Laffer had gone down, they would have had the services of a doctor. But with Laffer hurt, they didn't have that luxury.

"I think I've got the viewscreen working," Thorn announced. He made a few more adjustments to circumvent the damaged sensors. "Here goes."

In the next instant, the screen went from black to a blinding, coruscating blue, shot through with twisting, writhing cylinders of red. As the captain watched, the image changed. The blue became orange, the red cylinders a series of green spikes.

He had seen something like it on Earth once, during a summer vacation in Alaska. Their guides had called the phenomenon the northern lights. But of course, what Sisko saw now was much more vivid, much more beautiful.

And much more frightening, considering what it had done to them and their ship. With an effort, the captain tore his gaze from the screen and turned to Lopez.

"Esteban, what is it?"

The science officer didn't turn around. He just shrugged.

"Hard to say," he answered. "But whatever it is, it's sucking us into its center. And from what I can tell, the forces that tossed us about just now are even more tumultuous the deeper you go."

Sisko didn't like the sound of that. "Continue your investigation," he told Lopez. "I'll have Dax give you a hand as soon as she's done below."

He had barely completed his instructions when the turbolift doors opened and spit out the Trill. "Counselor Barnes and Lieutenant Zar are looking after Dr. Laffer," she announced, heading straight for one of the control stations. "I thought I'd be more help up here."

"I've asked Lieutenant Lopez to determine what we're up against," the captain said.

It was all the explanation she needed. As she set to work just a few feet from Lopez, the man glanced at her.

"I certainly chose one *hell* of a way to get close to you," he joked.

Dax looked up for a second. "It wasn't your fault," she pointed out.

"It was *my* turn at the helm," Lopez insisted. "I should've seen it coming, whatever it was."

The Trill frowned. "There'll be plenty of time to beat yourself up later," she told him. "Right now, we've got a job to do."

"Exactly," Sisko joined in.

At the sound of his voice, Dax glanced over her shoulder at him. He saw something strange in her eyes.

A need to speak, he realized. A desire to share some valuable bit of information. But the Trill's expression said it could wait awhile, just like Lopez's self-recriminations.

The captain looked up at the viewscreen, where the phenomenon danced and whirled in hues so rich they hurt his eyes. How could anything so lovely have placed them in such a bind? he wondered.

"Please," said Jangor, "sit down."

Odo complied, choosing a spot on a long, low couch covered in soft, dark fabric. As he sat, he sank several inches into the thing, so that his feet didn't quite reach the floor.

The expression on Rom's face told the constable how foolish he looked. But still, it wasn't polite to refuse a seat from one's trading partner. And Jangor himself was occupying the only other acceptable seat in the room, a big, high-backed wooden throne that he had no doubt pilfered from one of the more primitive worlds in the sector.

So the Ferengi sat down next to Odo—and sank in just as much. It was a source of perverse and unexpected satisfaction to the changeling that Rom's feet didn't reach the ground either.

"This is, er, a very nice place you've got here," Odo observed. After all, that's how Quark would have opened the conversation. Or so he believed.

"Thank you," Jangor replied. "Though, really, it's furnished much the same as my old ship. As you will recall, I am a creature of habit."

"Yes," Rom chuckled knowingly. "Very much a creature of habit."

The Retizian responded with the kind of look a Klingon might give a dull blade. Apparently he only tolerated Quark's brother. But then, it wasn't Rom who had saved his life all those years ago.

"May I offer you something to eat? To drink?" asked Jangor, turning to the being he thought was his old friend.

"No, thank you," Rom answered, speaking for both himself and Odo. "Perhaps later."

"Very well, then," Jangor said, leaning forward to emphasize his desire to converse with Quark. "So, you old dust devil, it appears you're interested in my power coils."

Rom set his hands on edge in his lap, palms together. That meant Odo was neither to agree nor disagree, but to act circumspect.

"You could say that," he told their host.

Jangor looked at him askance. "You're interested in something else, perhaps?"

Rom turned his hands palms down. The signal to disagree.

"No, not really," Odo replied.

"Then you *are* interested in the power coils," the Retizian concluded.

Rom's hands turned palms up. He pretended to inspect them.

"Yes," Odo said. "I am interested indeed."

He was getting the feeling their system of hand signals might end up hampering the negotiations. However, it was too late to change it now.

"I see," Jangor remarked. "And you have a market for these coils?"

Rom's palms remained up.

"That's correct," the changeling said.

The Retizian's eyes narrowed. "And might I ask what it is?"

Palms down.

"Now then," Odo responded, "I don't think that should be of any consequence. Particularly between old friends."

Jangor grunted. "Perhaps not. The only thing of real consequence, I suppose, is the price of the bargain."

Palms up.

The changeling nodded. "I agree completely."

"Good," said the Retizian. "Then let's get down to the nitty-gritty. The coils are ten bars of gold-pressed latinum apiece, ninety if you buy all ten. And believe me, that is not a deal I would offer just anyone."

Palms down.

"Unfortunately," Odo told him, "I had a slightly different figure in mind."

He wasn't sure what that figure might be, of course. But with luck, Rom would find a way to tell him.

"Different," Jangor repeated thoughtfully. He leaned back in his chair and tapped his fingers on the wooden armrest. *"How* different?"

The shapeshifter shrugged. "How different do you *think?"*

The Retizian eyed him critically. "For all ten?"

Odo didn't need Rom to provide the answer to that question. "All ten," he confirmed.

Jangor stroked his chin. "Eight and a half bars."

Palms down.

The constable sighed. "I was thinking of a somewhat *greater* difference."

"Greater," their host echoed. Jangor seemed to have lost much of his good humor.

Apparently the fact that Quark had saved his thieving hide counted for only so much. In that regard,

Odo suspected, Retizians and Ferengi had a great deal in common.

"Eight and a quarter," Jangor decided.

Rom's palms remained down. The changeling bit his lip. He could imagine few things more painful than this petty niggling.

Nonetheless he maintained his composure. After all, he reminded himself, he was doing this for Kira.

"I was hoping you could do better than that," Odo told the Retizian.

Jangor leaned even farther back into his seat. Clearly, he was finding this negotiation more nettlesome than he had expected.

"Better," the Retizian remarked dryly, managing to make the concept sound inherently unreasonable.

Rom turned his hands palms upward. It wasn't necessary, of course. The shapeshifter had recognized the remark as a rhetorical one.

Suddenly Jangor rose from his chair. One of his eyes was twitching, indicating the rise of volatile emotions within.

"Is there something wrong?" he asked Rom, his voice seething with pique.

The Ferengi looked up at him with the innocence of a newborn babe. "What do you mean?" he inquired.

"What I mean," said the Retizian, "is you've been fidgeting with your hands ever since you walked in here. I find it more than a little distracting to have to watch you."

Rom was clearly at a loss as to what to say. And

judging from the tone in Jangor's voice, there was a potential for things to get even worse.

"I agree," Odo said, getting to his feet to draw the Retizian's attention to himself. "My brother *can* be distracting, at times. Unfortunately, this quirk of his is neurological—and quite incurable." He turned to Rom. "Isn't that right, Brother?"

The Ferengi nodded meekly. "Yes, quite incurable."

The constable turned back to Jangor. "I apologize, old friend. The last thing I wanted to do was cause you discomfort."

The Retizian looked at him intently. Only after a while did his features begin to soften, then soften some more. Finally, taking a deep breath, Jangor receded into his high-backed chair.

"It's I who should apologize," he said. "There was a time when that sort of thing wouldn't have bothered me at all. Now . . ." He shook his head miserably. "Never grow old, my friend."

For a moment, there was silence in the wake of the Retizian's remark. In the end, Odo was the one who broke it.

"I have a suggestion," he declared. "Why don't we rest up and try this again tomorrow? I think we'll all be in a better frame of mind."

Jangor thought for a moment, then nodded. "I believe you're right, Quark." He managed a smile. "You always were the voice of reason, weren't you?"

The changeling fashioned a smile of his own. "Now

that you mention it," he said, "I believe I was. And a good thing for you, Fel Jangor."

The Retizian chuckled. "Yes, a good thing for me. Tomorrow then?"

Odo nodded. "Tomorrow it is."

With a perfunctory wave of his hand, Jangor started to leave the room. Then he looked back at his visitors.

"Where are my manners?" he asked. "That ship you came on can't be very comfortable. Why don't you spend the night on my vessel, so we can get an early start in the morning?"

Out of the corner of his eye, the constable could see Rom starting to turn his hands palms upward. Fortunately the Ferengi thought better of it. Instead, he just stared at his "brother," as if hoping to get the message across by means of telepathy.

Not being telepathic, however, Odo could only guess at the right response. What's more, he didn't have a great deal of time in which to do so.

He looked up at the Retizian. "We . . . would be delighted."

"Good," said Jangor. "I'll have one of my servants see to your accommodations." Then he left the room.

Once he was certain that their host was gone, the changeling turned to Rom. The Ferengi held his hands up in an appeal for forgiveness.

"Sorry," he whined, for good measure.

"Sorry indeed," muttered Odo.

Clearly they would have to find another way to

make this work, or Kira's friends could forget about their power coils.

In the wardroom of the *Defiant*, Sisko sat back in his seat, surveyed those assembled around the table, and sighed. He was just beginning to get a handle on how bad things really were.

"So Dr. Laffer's condition may be even worse than we thought?" he asked Counselor Barnes.

"It seems that way," she confirmed. "Without a doctor on hand, it's hard to tell for certain. And if she takes a turn for the worse, none of us here is really qualified to deal with it."

The captain nodded. "I see." He turned to O'Brien and Graal, who sat next to each other. "And the propulsion system?"

The chief scowled. "It's a mess."

"How long to get the warp drive working again?" Sisko inquired.

O'Brien glanced at the Craynid, then shrugged. "A couple of days, maybe. Certainly not less than a day and a half."

The captain grunted and looked to Zar. "Lieutenant?"

"I got a distress call out," the Bolian reported. "But we're pretty far from any other Federation vessels. I'm not optimistic that we'll receive help on a timely basis."

Sisko made a pyramid of his hands and turned his attention to Thorn. "What about the shields?" he asked. "Don't tell me there's bad news from that quarter as well."

"I won't," replied the security chief. "Fortunately the shields are working fine. We're fully protected from any and all radiation hazards—at least for the time being."

The captain smiled. "Thank you, Mr. Thorn. I could always count on you in a pinch." Finally, he eyed Dax and Lopez. "Well? Any idea what it is we've blundered into?"

"We have a theory," the Trill began.

"Yes," said Lopez. "Our sensor information indicates we're situated at the nexus of two sets of energy waves—each one generated by a supernova in the area."

"I know how unlikely that sounds," Dax added quickly. "Nonetheless, it's the truth."

"Why didn't we detect this sooner?" asked Sisko.

"We would have," Lopez answered, "if we'd been traveling at sublight. But, of course, we weren't. And this nexus is virtually undetectable at warp speeds."

"The worse news," Dax remarked soberly, "is that we're being drawn deeper and deeper into the thing— even more quickly than we first suspected. In ten hours, maybe less, the stresses on the *Defiant* will be great enough to tear her apart."

Her announcement was met with an oppressive silence. The captain surveyed the faces of his colleagues, old and new. None of them looked very happy about the situation.

But then, they had all been in worse spots than this one. Somehow they would find a way out of it.

"Clearly," he said, "we've got to escape this phenomenon before we reach the point of no return—and we don't have time to repair the warp drive." He looked to O'Brien. "Any chance of repairing those escape pods, Chief?"

It was Graal who replied first. "That is not an option," she noted. "The damage is too severe."

Sisko cursed inwardly. "All right, then. What about the impulse engines? Can we get them working in the next several hours—say, at even partial effectiveness?"

The chief frowned. "I don't know, sir."

"We will make the attempt," the Craynid elaborated. "But there are no guarantees."

"I wasn't expecting any," the captain told her. "Take Mr. Thorn with you. Maybe he'll see something you've overlooked."

Judging from O'Brien's expression, he didn't think that was very likely. Nonetheless, he nodded. "Aye, sir."

Sisko turned to Zar and Barnes. "You two will have to look after Dr. Laffer. Take turns, two hours apiece or whatever you're comfortable with. But stay alert in case her status changes."

The Bolian would have liked to be more involved in the rehabilitation of ship's systems. The captain knew that. But he also knew that Zar would follow orders, no matter what they were.

"Aye, sir," said the Bolian. Barnes just nodded.

"What about me?" asked Lopez.

Sisko looked at him. "See what you can do about repairing the sensor array, Esteban. We may need it at full capacity before we're done."

The captain was about to ask Dax to work alongside the science officer. But when he saw her expression, he thought better of it.

"You're with me," he told the Trill.

There was a spark of gratitude in her eyes. "Aye, Captain."

No one wondered where Sisko and Dax were going or what they were doing. After all, everyone had his or her own assignment to attend to, and that was more than enough to worry about for the time being.

But the captain wondered. Fortunately, he thought, it wouldn't be long before he found out.

CHAPTER
10

JAKE COULDN'T HELP but be aware of how empty his quarters felt without his father around. He had hoped having Nog over for a Fretillian fizz would change that. Unfortunately Nog wasn't very good company lately.

"He's in trouble," said the Ferengi, leaning back into Sisko's couch. "I know he is."

Jake shook his head. "You don't know that. Your father might be doing a great job."

Nog grunted. "I know my father. And I tell you, he is not doing a great job at all. Despite his good intentions, he may throw a . . ." He paused, searching for the right idiom.

"A what?" asked the human.

"You know," said the Ferengi, looking annoyed. "An implement used by animals or something—

small, hairy animals with bowlegs. You said they were your ancestors, though I think you were joking."

Jake thought for a moment. Finally it came to him. "A monkey wrench," he announced triumphantly.

"Yes," said Nog, pointing at him. "A monkey wrench, exactly. That is what my father will throw into the negotiations."

The human sighed. "You've got to have confidence in him, Nog—the same way you would want him to have confidence in you."

The Ferengi peered up at him. "You don't understand. My father is putting his career on the line—maybe even his life."

Jake looked at him askance. "His *life?* What do you mean?"

Nog scowled. "I mean my father hasn't exactly impressed anyone with his ability to transact business. And a Ferengi without a head for business has no future. He might as well be dead."

The human scowled back at him. "You really believe that?"

Nog gnawed pensively on one of his knuckles. "No," he said at last. "Not really. But all the rest of my people believe it, so what difference does it make what I think?"

"It makes a lot of difference," Jake insisted. "I don't think your father cares all that much what other Ferengi think. But I think he'd be hurt if he thought he'd disappointed *you.*"

His friend pondered the advice. After a while, it

seemed to comfort him. "I suppose you're right," he said, "in a hu-man kind of way."

Jake smiled. "That's the only way I know."

"You know," said Nog, cheering up visibly, "I think I could use another fizz. How about you?"

The boy nodded. "Sure. I'll get us a couple."

The Ferengi held his hand up. "No. This round is on me."

He looked scared for a moment, as he realized what he'd said. Instantly he amended it.

"That's a figure of speech, of course."

"Of course," Jake assured him.

He watched Nog enter the cooking area. The Ferengi didn't often offer to serve anyone—he always said he did too much of that in his uncle's bar. So this was a rare occasion.

And maybe, the human thought, a small expression of Nog's gratitude. Not that it was necessary. Jake wasn't looking for thanks. Seeing his friend's spirits improve was reward enough.

Besides, talking about Rom's predicament made the captain's seem petty by comparison. Nog's father was involved in a tricky situation, with his reputation hanging in the balance.

Jake's dad was only coping with a difficult memory—and from the looks of things before he left, it wasn't as difficult as Jake had feared. In fact, his trip to Mars might even have turned out to be fun.

The boy shook his head at the irony. Here he'd been

worried sick about the captain's reaction to his old colleagues—and it was Rom who was turning out to have all the trouble on his hands.

It just goes to show you, he mused, as Nog finished mixing the fizzes and brought them over. Things are hardly ever what they seem.

Sisko waited until the door to his quarters had slid closed, leaving him alone with Dax. Then he turned to her.

"So?" he prodded. "What did you want to see me about, Old Man?"

Dax frowned. "What happened to those escape pods wasn't just bad luck. We've got a saboteur on our hands, Benjamin."

He nodded. "Yes, I know that."

She looked at him, surprised. "You know?" she asked.

"I know," the captain confirmed. "O'Brien and Graal came to me a little while ago. They said that just before we fell victim to the wave nexus, they found a sabotaged damper node."

Dax grunted. "You might have shared that with me, Benjamin."

Sisko shrugged. "I would have if the opportunity had presented itself. But we've been too busy until now."

The Trill took a breath and let it out. "All right, I forgive you."

"Thanks," the captain replied. "Now, we ought to—"

She held up her hand. "Hang on a minute. I'm not done."

"Oh?" he responded. What else did she have to tell him?

"I think I know who the saboteur *is,*" Dax went on.

Now it was *his* turn to be surprised. "Really," he said. "Well, don't keep me in suspense, dammit."

Dax folded her arms across her chest, as if she weren't entirely comfortable with her conclusion. How could she be?

"It's Thorn," she told him.

Sisko swallowed. It had hurt to know that one of his former colleagues was up to no good. But to hear a name put to the crime . . .

"You have evidence?" he asked.

The Trill pressed her lips together, then shook her head. "Not exactly. Remember, I said I *think* I know who it is. But it's not conclusive."

Inwardly the captain felt relieved. "Why don't you tell me about it anyway, and let me judge for myself?"

"All right," she agreed. "When we were on the bridge together, Thorn lied to me. He said he'd served on the *Victory.* Well, as it happened, I knew someone else who'd served on the *Victory.* A Vulcan named Simora, who came through *Deep Space Nine* on the *Wellington.*"

Sisko recalled the *Wellington*'s stopover. "Go on."

Dax did as she was instructed. "When I asked Thorn if he knew Simora, he said yes. But he went on to describe her as unfriendly to humans—not an uncommon appearance when it comes to Vulcans.

145

After all, most of them are rather standoffish with regard to other species."

"But?" the captain provided.

"But Simora was an exception," she told him. "She got along fine with everyone, humans included. And Thorn would have known that—if he was telling the truth."

Sisko absorbed the information. "I know for a fact," he said, "that Thorn served on the *Victory*. It's in his service file. So why would the man lie about knowing this friend of yours?"

"I don't know," the Trill told him. "But there's more, Benjamin. You see, it was Thorn who laid in the course that brought us to the nexus. If he had varied even a fraction of a degree, we would have missed it." She looked at him. "You see what I mean?"

The captain couldn't help but see it. However, it was still hard to believe. Aidan Thorn was one of the finest, bravest, most trustworthy men he'd ever known. At least, he'd always thought so—until now.

"But why would he have done all this?" Sisko asked, posing the question to himself as much as to Dax. "What did he have to gain? I mean, we're all in this together. If we perish here, Thorn will perish, too."

His friend shook her head. "I'll admit," she remarked, "it's a mystery why he or anyone else would want to see us stranded. But *someone* is responsible. And it looks to me like Thorn's the one."

The captain sighed. He hated this. He wanted to deny it with every fiber of his being. However, he couldn't let his personal feelings get in the way of his crew's survival.

"If you want," Dax offered, "I'll keep an eye on him. With any luck, he'll give us some idea of what he's up to—before our ten hours are up."

"That won't be necessary," Sisko told her. "I've got O'Brien and Graal on the case already." He indicated the corridor with a tilt of his head. "Now let's make ourselves useful before we're missed."

"We need to implement a change of strategy," Odo decided, pacing the length of the quarters that Jangor had assigned to them.

"I'm ashamed of myself," said Rom, cradling his head in his hands. "I'm more than ashamed, I'm mortified."

The constable stopped. "Did you hear what I said?" he asked.

"My brother's right," the Ferengi went on. "I'm a third-rate negotiator, a disgrace to my family and everyone I've ever been associated with."

Odo rolled his eyes. He had no intention of listening to this drivel. Not when they had to figure out a way to salvage their operation.

"Try to get hold of yourself," he told his companion. "We made a mistake, that's all. Now we're going to do better."

But Rom seemed determined to flagellate himself.

"My brother told me over and over," he moaned. "I just don't have the knack that he has. I'm a failure at business."

The shapeshifter sighed. *Now he tells me he's a failure. Why couldn't he have said that in the beginning? Why couldn't he have warned me that he would crack under the pressure?*

Unfortunately Odo was stuck with him. If he didn't want to disappoint Kira, he would just have to make the best of it.

"I have no right calling myself a Ferengi," Rom complained. "A Ferengi without profit . . ."

"Is no Ferengi at all," the changeling finished, without really thinking about it.

Rom looked up at him, momentarily halted in his chant of self-deprecation. "The eighteenth Rule of Acquisition. Very good."

Odo scowled. "As I was saying, we need to try a different approach—one that doesn't rely on hand signals. Or, for that matter, any other kind of signal."

The Ferengi seemed puzzled. "But without signals, how will you know what to do? What to say?"

"Simple," said the constable. "I'll wing it."

O'Brien looked at Graal, then Thorn, and frowned. "All right," he said. "You heard the captain. We need to get this vessel up and running in the next several hours—or else."

Tapping a padd on one of the consoles, he brought up a schematic of the impulse engines on the monitor directly above. As he had indicated in the wardroom, the things were a mess.

"This is what we've got to work with," he told his colleagues. "And these are in *good* shape compared to the warp drive. As you can see, we've got our work cut out for us."

At his right shoulder, the Craynid made a whistling sound. Thorn, looking over O'Brien's left shoulder, just grunted.

"I'm no propulsion expert," the big man remarked, "but it seems several engine components went completely undamaged."

"That's true," the chief agreed. "Unfortunately several other components were turned to junk—especially the smaller, more delicate parts. And we need all of them to get ourselves moving again."

Thorn scowled. "If they're as small as they look, why can't we simply make more of them with our replicators? Surely their patterns are in the ship's computer somewhere."

O'Brien thought for a moment. "Interesting idea," he conceded. "But there's a bit of a problem. To replace all the parts, we'd need more raw material than we have on board."

"Then why not replicate the most crucial components," Graal suggested, "and replace the rest with parts from other systems?" She pointed to the screen. "This, for instance. The wave modulation spur. With a little work, we can substitute a graviton inverter from the tractor assembly."

The chief looked at her. "You might have something there," he told her. Turning to his control panel, he did a few quick calculations. Then he smiled. "You might indeed."

"I will seek out the necessary specifications for the replicators," the Craynid volunteered.

Thorn looked at her. "I'll give you a hand."

O'Brien nodded. "Good." He tapped his communicator badge. "Engineering to Captain Sisko."

"Sisko here," came the reply. "What have you got, Chief?"

"An idea," O'Brien began. "But it'll be a while before we know if it's going to work. Basically we're talking about replicating replacement parts for the impulse engines—and jury-rigging the rest."

There was a pause. Apparently the captain had his doubts about their approach. But on the other hand, he seemed to respect their opinions.

"Keep me posted," he told O'Brien.

"Will do," the chief responded. "O'Brien out."

In the room they'd been given on Fel Jangor's ship, Odo watched Rom's jaw drop. It was not the most attractive thing he had ever seen.

"You'll wing it?" echoed Quark's brother. "But how? You're not a Ferengi. You haven't been trained in the delicate art of negotiation."

"Then train me," the constable told him.

Rom looked appalled. "Here? Now?"

"Why not?" asked Odo. "I've already memorized the Rules of Acquisition."

The Ferengi shook his head sadly. "The Rules of Acquisition are only the most basic guidelines. To negotiate a deal effectively, you need style. You need panache."

"Like Quark?" the shapeshifter inquired.

Rom nodded vigorously. "Oh yes. My brother has a great deal of style."

"All right," said Odo. "Then it's just a matter of my adopting it. If you can tell me how Quark operates, I'll take it from there."

The Ferengi looked hesitant. "Quark wouldn't like my telling you about him. Not at all."

"Why not?" asked the constable.

Rom's lips pressed together tightly. "He just wouldn't. It's kind of . . ." He shrugged. "Kind of personal."

"I see," said Odo. "And how personally will Quark take it if I shut down his bar for a few weeks? Say, because of some minor health code infractions I've seen fit to overlook until now?"

The Ferengi swallowed at the prospect. "You wouldn't."

The shapeshifter smiled. "Oh, wouldn't I?"

Rom sighed. "Then again," he replied, "perhaps my brother would understand if I gave you a few small pointers."

"Such as?" Odo prodded.

"Well," said the Ferengi, "according to my brother, the key to being a good negotiator is acting as if you don't care if the deal falls through." For emphasis he made a gesture of dismissal.

The constable looked at him uncertainly. "But I *do* care," he explained. "These power coils are very important to Kira and her people."

"Of course they are," Rom told him. "But Quark would say to forget all that, if you want to succeed."

Odo harrumphed. "Maybe that works for Quark, but it's not going to work for me. Maybe I should learn some other style of negotiation—something more suited to my temperament."

Rom grunted uncomfortably. "Pardon me for saying so, but I don't know any Ferengi with your temperament."

The changeling scowled. "All right, then. Forget my temperament. Just run through some classic strategies and I'll pick one."

His companion thought for a moment. "Well," he said at last, "there's the Moxon Maneuver. That's often effective."

"The Moxon Maneuver? What's that?" asked Odo.

"It was named after my father's uncle Moxon," Rom explained. "When he would enter a negotiation with someone who didn't know him, he would pretend to be stupid." The Ferengi made loops in the air around his ears and crossed his eyes. "You know, mentally incapable."

The shapeshifter regarded him. "And this was an asset?"

Rom nodded enthusiastically. "Oh yes. It caused whomever he was dealing with to lower their guards. They were so eager to take advantage of Uncle

Moxon, they ended up agreeing to a bad transaction. Bad for them, that is—not for Uncle Moxon."

Odo shook his head. "I don't think I'd be very good at playing dumb. And also, Jangor knows Quark. He wouldn't know what to make of it if I began acting out of character."

The Ferengi frowned. "That's true."

"What else is there?" the changeling inquired.

Again Rom gave the problem some thought. Finally, his eyes lit up. "There's always the Pluboi Ploy."

"Pluboi?" Odo repeated. "Another uncle, I suppose?"

"A distant cousin," the Ferengi told him. "On my Moogie's side, bless her tiny lobes."

"Charming," said the constable. "And what's *his* angle?"

Rom smiled. "Information overload. Pluboi makes a point of having prodigious amounts of data on any subject you can name. And when a deal comes up, he makes it available to whomever wants it."

Odo's eyes narrowed. Actually, he thought, it was a rather clever approach. "The other negotiators are so flooded with information, they don't know what to believe. Then your cousin moves in and capitalizes on their confusion."

The Ferengi snickered and rubbed his hands together. "Exactly. So, er . . . what do you think?"

The shapeshifter shook his head. "It's a little too late to start accumulating data on power coils. And even if we could get our hands on some, I've got a feeling Jangor wouldn't fall for it. He seems too sure of himself to be swayed by that sort of tactic."

"You know," said Rom, "I had a feeling you were going to say that. Unfortunately it doesn't leave us much else." Suddenly, his eyes opened wide and he snapped his fingers. "Except the Krechma Offensive!"

Odo eyed him. "And what's that?"

"Krechma—who, I regret to say, is not at all related to me—was one of our most brilliant negotiators until his life ended several years ago in a strip-mining accident." The Ferengi paused. "It was suspicious, too—the way he died, I mean. To this day, there are those who insist he wasn't checking the treads on that vehicle at all, but—"

"Rom!" the changeling snarled.

The Ferengi stopped dead in his tracks. "Sorry," he said earnestly. "I guess I get carried away sometimes."

"You don't have to apologize." Odo sighed. "Just tell me about this Krechma person, will you?"

"Right," Rom replied, waxing serious. "You see, Krechma's strategy was to instill fear in his adversaries. He would do it any way he could—by making them think their goods were substandard, by implying there was a competitor entering the market, whatever he could think of."

"Fear," the constable echoed. "And it worked?"

"Like a charm," the Ferengi swore. "In a matter of minutes, Krechma could find your worst fear and amplify it. Before long, your nerves would be so jangled, you would give him whatever he wanted—

and thank him profusely for taking it." He grinned. "You can see why Krechma is one of my heroes."

Odo didn't respond to the remark. He simply considered the possibilities—and ultimately rejected them.

"Too idiosyncratic," he concluded. "It would take a special sort of personality to elicit that kind of result. And as I noted before, Jangor is a seasoned negotiator. I believe even someone like Krechma—were he alive today—would have a hard time with our host."

Rom shrugged. "I can't think of anything else. Oh, there are plenty of other approaches, I'm sure—but when it comes to negotiation, my people don't generally advertise their tactics."

"No," said the shapeshifter, "I don't suppose they would. That leaves only one other option open to me."

"And what's that?" asked his companion.

Odo lifted his chin in a show of determination. "I'll have to develop a style of my *own.*"

For two hours, Zar had assisted Lopez in his attempts to repair the *Defiant*'s hobbled sensor array. While they had made some progress, there was still a long way to go.

The Bolian would have liked to stay with his old colleague, to see their efforts through to completion. Unfortunately that wasn't in the cards. Captain Sisko had asked him to take turns with Barnes watching over Dr. Laffer, and Zar never disobeyed an order.

Except that once, of course. But if he hadn't, Sisko

would have fallen victim to the Borg—and by that time, there had been plenty of victims already.

As he entered sickbay, Zar found Barnes standing beside Laffer, arms folded tightly across her chest. The counselor appeared helpless, frustrated. When she looked up at him, there were shadows beneath her eyes—and not from lack of sleep, he intimated.

The doctor, of course, looked worse. Much worse.

"Anything to report?" the Bolian asked softly.

Barnes shook her head. "Everything's the same."

"It's my shift," Zar reminded her. "Why don't you go lie down for a little while? Or see if there's something you can do up on the bridge?"

The counselor nodded. "I guess I could use the change of scenery."

"Go ahead," he told her. "The doctor and I will be fine."

That got a smile out of her, albeit a sad one. "I'm sure you will," she replied.

With obvious reluctance, she made her way around Laffer's biobed and headed for the exit. But a moment later, she was gone.

The Bolian turned to his old colleague, whose pallor was hard to ignore. He sighed. "I don't mind baby-sitting for you this once," he told her. "Just let's not make a habit of it."

Laffer had never responded much to his jokes. She didn't respond now, either. Sighing, Zar found a chair and settled into it. He could see it was going to be a long vigil.

CHAPTER
11

QUARK OPENED HIS eyes, looked around, and groaned. He was in the infirmary on *Deep Space Nine*, of all places. And he felt absolutely awful.

His head felt as if it had been packed with sand. Aside from being very uncomfortable, the sensation made it dreadfully hard to think. He groaned a second time, even louder than the first.

"Nice sound," said Bashir.

Craning his neck, the Ferengi saw the doctor approaching from the other side of the medical facility. He had a tricorder in his hand.

"If I didn't know better," Bashir continued, "I would have thought I had a pregnant mugato on my hands."

Quark looked at him. "A mugato?" he echoed.

"What in the hallowed name of the Grand Nagus is that?"

"The mugato," said the doctor, as he ran his tricorder over the Ferengi, "is a primate on—"

Quark interrupted with a wave of his hand. "I've changed my mind," he declared. "I don't really want to know. Just tell me what the hell I'm doing *here*—when just a moment ago I was on Risa." He recalled the place with infinite longing. "It was a pristine beach, with white sand and sighing soja trees and the most exquisite turquoise sea. I was setting up a consortium to turn the place into a lithium-cracking station . . ."

The doctor smiled that insufferable smile of his. Quark frowned. Ferengi physicians didn't bother with such pleasantries. Why bother when no one wanted to pay extra for a bedside manner?

"Well," said Bashir, "I see you're ahead of schedule. You weren't supposed to wake up for another couple of hours yet." He picked up Quark's hand and examined it. "The spots are fading as well."

The Ferengi looked at him. "Spots? What spots?" Withdrawing his hand, he inspected it himself—and gasped. *"Gruw'r!"* he gasped.

"So it would seem," the doctor agreed. "Of course, it's in its latter stages. You're no longer in any real danger."

Quark breathed a sigh of relief. He'd always known the disease would catch up with him sometime. Apparently it had done just that.

But then . . . what about the beach on Risa? Had

all that been a dream, brought on by the ravages of the disease?

"How long have I been here?" he asked.

Bashir shrugged. "About twenty-four hours. Your brother found you unconscious in your quarters and called for help."

The Ferengi smiled. "That Rom. Always around when I need him." A dark and disturbing thought came to him. "Wait a minute. He's not robbing me blind while I lie here, is he?" Quark tried to sit up, but found he was too weak and plunked back down again. "Stop him, Doctor," he breathed. "Please—while there's still time!"

Bashir shook his head. "Rom's not robbing you. I can assure you of that. In fact, your bar's been closed ever since he left."

Quark looked at him. "Since he *left?* Where in blazes did he go?"

The doctor regarded him. "You don't remember? The power coils for that village on Bajor? The meeting with your friend Fel Jangor?"

Suddenly it all came back to him, flooding his mind like a swarm of darting jinga wasps. Not the black kind, either, but the white ones—whose stings hurt for days.

"Major Kira is going to kill me," the Ferengi moaned.

"I wouldn't worry about it," said Bashir.

Quark grasped him by the arm. "You don't understand. My brother doesn't know the first thing about negotiation. He'll fall right on his face."

"Perhaps," the doctor replied. "But as I understand it, Rom isn't the one doing the negotiating."

The Ferengi looked at him. "Then who *is?*"

"It's Odo," Bashir told him.

At first Quark didn't believe him. Then, even through the fog brought on by the disease, he realized what must have taken place.

In fact, he realized even more than that. Because if the constable was away, impersonating him, and most everyone else in authority was gone with the captain to Mars . . .

"I've got to open the bar," the Ferengi announced.

He tried to sit up again. However, the doctor placed his hand on Quark's chest and prevented him from doing so.

"Not now you're not," Bashir informed him. "You may be well on the road to recovery, but you're not there yet."

"But every minute I stay here—"

"Is a squandering of potential profits," the doctor noted. "I'm well aware of that. But if I release you too early, there could be complications, and I'm sure neither of us wants that."

Quark cursed beneath his breath. "You don't call a loss of business a complication?" He moaned. "How am I supposed to get my health back when everything I care about is in jeopardy? How am I supposed to convalesce when my mind is in such awful turmoil?"

The doctor looked at him askance. "There's nothing I like better than a little hyperbole, my friend—

and once again, you've proven your talent for it. However, that talent notwithstanding, you're going to remain here until I tell you otherwise. Case closed."

The Ferengi bit his lip. "I demand to see Major Kira. She understands tyranny. She'll get me out of here."

"Perhaps," Bashir said amiably. "But last I looked, the ranking physician on a Federation facility has the last word in matters of health." He smiled sympathetically. "I'm afraid you've no recourse but to remain here, Quark. You might as well accept it."

The Ferengi tried to get up a third time, but it was clear he didn't have the strength. In fact, he found himself getting light-headed from the effort. Settling back, he did as the doctor had advised.

He accepted his confinement—at least for the time being. But by the Nagus's great and glorious lobes, he wouldn't accept it much longer.

Constance Barnes tried her best to negotiate the corridor outside the *Defiant*'s sickbay, but it wasn't as easy as it should have been.

The bulkheads seemed to buckle, spewing clouds of sparks like demons out of childhood fantasies. Flames leapt ahead and behind her, lashing her skin with their unholy heat. Even the deck beneath her feet became shifting and unreliable, aquiver with deep rumblings from the bowels of the ship.

No, she told herself, holding her hands out to either side for balance. She closed her eyes as tightly as she could, shutting out the sight of the sparks and the flames. It's not real, she insisted. None of it is real. It's just another waking nightmare.

Barnes had had lots of them on the *Endeavor*. At first, they were just spikes of anxiety, eerie and unexpected echoes of the terror she had felt on the *Saratoga*. Then they became progressively worse—darker, more vivid, more disturbing—until she was afraid to sleep for fear they'd overwhelm her.

She had been able to get some sleeping medication from the *Endeavor*'s chief medical officer—a friend of hers. But that hadn't helped her when the attacks came during the day. And despite the horror and the insanity of her episodes, she was forced to pretend everything was all right—or the captain would have stripped her of her responsibilities as ship's counselor.

And she couldn't abide that—not at all. She had a duty. She had a *mission*, for god sakes, grim as it might be. And she couldn't let anyone or anything turn her away from it.

Opening her eyes, she saw that the flames and the sparks had gone away. The bulkheads were no longer buckling and the deck had been restored to normal. Everything was as it should be again.

Safe. Familiar. Unthreatening.

Taking a deep breath, she started down the corridor anew. One step at a time, each with a little more assurance than the one before it. Soon a spectator would have believed there was nothing wrong with her.

It was important for everyone to believe that. It was important that she fool them as she had fooled Captain Kyprios.

Certainly the captain had sensed her discomfort with the idea of a reunion with her former shipmates. But he had failed to understand the depth of her pain, or the nature of it.

It wasn't dread she felt when she got wind of the christening of the new *Saratoga*. It was a need, an emptiness she had to fill—a yearning so powerful she could barely tolerate it.

Finally, after all these years, she had a chance to free herself of her raging, shambling nightmares. And she wouldn't blow it. She promised herself that with feverish intensity.

Not that it would be easy. In fact, it was already the most difficult thing she had done in her entire life. But she swore to herself she would find the strength to see it through. She would—

Suddenly the deck pitched beneath her feet again. As she fought for balance, darkness fell. Structural supports shrieked like souls in hideous torment all around her.

A section of bulkhead blew out into the corridor, releasing an angry confusion of electromagnetic tendrils that writhed like emerald wraiths. The air grew thick and stifling with the stench of blood and charred flesh and metal grinding on metal.

No, she thought. It's happening again, worse than before—worse than ever. Just like on the *Saratoga*.

Fear clutched at her throat, at her heart, and

squeezed until she could barely breathe. Closing her eyes, clamping her hands over her ears, she lunged forward, unable to bear it any longer.

Somewhere up ahead was a turbolift, and the promise of deliverance from her madness. If I can only reach the bridge, she told herself, I'll be all right. *If I can only reach the bridge . . .*

Dax checked her monitors, worked at her controls, and scowled. It wasn't easy working with a sensor array at less than seventy-percent efficiency—and the sense of urgency around her made the job doubly difficult.

Nonetheless she had made good progress, accumulating a great deal of data via extended sweeps of the phenomenon. What's more, she was transmitting the information at intervals, trying to punch her way through the forces that roiled around them—so even if they perished, there was at least a slim chance their findings would survive.

Some people would have taken cold comfort in that, but the Trill was a Starfleet officer. One of her most important jobs was to expand the Federation's knowledge and understanding of celestial phenomena, and this nexus they were caught in certainly qualified.

Not that Dax would have *chosen* to give her life for such data. But if her life was going to be forfeit anyway, she was going to try her damnedest to leave something behind.

"How are we doing, Old Man?"

Turning, she saw the source of the question. It was the captain, of course, standing behind her. No one else in the galaxy called her "Old Man."

She basked in the familiarity of his presence. "I must've been pretty absorbed for you to sneak up on me, Benjamin."

Sisko shrugged. "I've snuck up on some of the best in my day. And that includes Curzon, if you recall."

She recalled, all right. It had been a training drill. Tough, demanding—and absolutely mandatory at the time for anyone who expected to be dealing with the Klingons.

"Doesn't it count that he was hung over?" the Trill asked.

"I was hung over myself," the captain reminded her. "I don't see that as much of an excuse."

Putting his hand on her shoulder, he leaned past her to check her monitors. The results were reflected in his eyes.

"Not bad," he said, "even for you."

Dax smiled grimly. "Thanks. I just hope it doesn't turn out to be my legacy, if you know what I mean."

"I do," he assured her.

Up on the viewscreen, the phenomenon's colors had actually intensified. For a moment, waves of purple and yellow predominated, only to be upstaged by a pattern of green blossoms—or anyway, what the Trill couldn't help but think of as blossoms. As they unfolded and grew, they turned orange and then red, then gave way to a series of blue oscillations.

"Not only fascinating," she said out loud, "but

esthetically pleasing as well. I doubt there's a race in the Federation who wouldn't appreciate this sight."

He nodded. "No argument here."

"Any sign of a response to our distress call?" the Trill asked.

Still intent on the screen, the captain shook his head. "Not any more than you'd expect. Even if it reached someone, it's too soon to hope for a return message. And before long, the energies swirling around us will cut off communications altogether." He glanced back at her. "As if you needed me to tell you that."

Dax regarded her friend. Despite the terrible gravity of their situation, despite the immense pressure on all of them, he seemed to be the very picture of serenity.

But then, that was the man's greatest strength—his rock-solid steadiness, his ability to keep his head in the midst of chaos. It was a quality much in demand right now.

"Well," said Sisko, "carry on. And if I hear anything, I promise you'll be the first to know."

"I'm going to hold you to that," the Trill told him.

Before he could straighten, however, the lift doors opened behind them. Out of casual curiosity, Dax turned to see who was joining them. After all, her shift wasn't over yet.

As it turned out, it was Counselor Barnes. But the woman looked angry, somehow. Or scared. Or both. And she was looking right at Dax.

"What the hell is the matter with you?" the counselor rasped, her eyes wide and red with reproval.

"I beg your pardon?" said the Trill, genuinely confused.

"What are you, some kind of monster?" Barnes demanded.

Dax shook her head. She still didn't get it. "Is this a joke?" she asked, thinking it wasn't very funny.

The counselor's mouth twisted with disgust. "We're all going to die in a few hours, don't you know that? And you sit there calmly gathering your data, like nothing's going on. Don't you have any feelings? Don't you *care?*"

Sisko frowned. "The lieutenant has just as many feelings as anyone else," he replied evenly. "What she's doing is valuable work—especially when her data may help others steer clear of such phenomena."

The counselor shook her head without even looking at him. "No," she said. Still fixed on Dax, her eyes were hollow, accusing. "That's scientific claptrap. You're no better than the Borg, you hear me? No better than the damned Borg!"

The Trill had heard just about enough. She understood that Barnes was under pressure. But hell, they were *all* under pressure—and no one else was getting quite so testy about it.

"Listen," she snapped, "I'm in no mood for this. If I were you, I'd find a nice, secluded seat somewhere and cool off."

She hadn't intended to make things worse—to

throw fuel on the fire. But the tone of her voice said otherwise. Barnes's eyes opened even wider as she advanced on Dax.

"Or what?" Barnes asked, leaning forward and planting her hand on the Trill's console. "Is that a threat, Lieutenant? Because if it is, you can be sure I won't back down from it."

"Take it any way you like," Dax told her, anger rising in her like an inexorable tide. The counselor was getting much too close for comfort. "Just get out of my way and let me do my job."

"Now just a damned minute here!" the captain barked. Interposing himself between the two women, he glowered at one and then the other. "This is the bridge of a starship—*my* starship—not an anbo-jytsu arena. If you want to chew each other out, do it somewhere else!"

Immediately Barnes's expression changed. Her eyes softening, her forehead smoothing over, she went from rampaging hostility to almost childlike regret in less than a heartbeat.

"Well?" Sisko demanded.

"I—I'm sorry," the counselor said, visibly shaken. She seemed as if she were trying to gather control of herself. "I'm so sorry."

Seeing her pain, the captain relented. "Are you all right?" he asked.

Barnes nodded. "I just lost my head. I don't know where all that anger came from." She regarded the Trill repentantly. "And unfortunately Lieutenant Dax was the nearest target."

Taking a breath, the Trill turned to Sisko. "It was my fault as well, Benjamin. I could've had a little more patience—been a little more understanding." She looked at Barnes and managed a smile of truce. "I guess we're all under a lot of strain right now."

"We are," the woman agreed. She looked mortified—a complete turnaround from her earlier demeanor. "But I'm a ship's counselor, for god sakes. I should be working to reduce the strain, not contributing to it."

The captain put a hand on Barnes's shoulder. "Go back to your quarters," he told her. "Get some rest."

The woman held a hand up to decline the offer. "It's all right," she assured him. "I'm fine now, really."

Sisko shook his head, his eyes hard and unyielding. "That wasn't a suggestion, Counselor. It was an order."

Barnes hesitated for a moment, as if she was going to put up a fight. Then she gave in. "If you say so, sir."

Something seemed to soften in the captain. "I do," he replied sympathetically. "What's more, I'm going to escort you there myself." He turned to Dax. "You have the conn, Lieutenant."

The Trill nodded. "Aye, sir."

The counselor looked a little embarrassed as Sisko guided her toward the turbolift. But she didn't resist.

Dax watched them disappear into the lift. Then she took a breath and turned back to her monitors.

It was strange how Barnes's tirade had seemed to come out of nowhere. Of course, she had been watching over Dr. Laffer, and that had to be a grim detail. But still, the woman was a ship's counselor—she had said so herself. She wasn't supposed to crack so easily.

Shrugging, the Trill turned back to her sensor investigation. If there was some other reason for Barnes to blow a gasket, Dax certainly wasn't aware of it.

Maybe the captain could figure it out.

CHAPTER
12

TRYING TO IGNORE the usual bustle around her in Ops, Kira regarded the image on her compact station monitor. The face that looked back at her wasn't at all a happy one.

"The Ferengi is *sick?*" Obahr echoed.

The major nodded. "Dr. Bashir is looking after him in the infirmary even as we speak."

The city administrator shook his head ruefully. "Then we've got no hope of acquiring those power coils, Nerys. We may as well start laying out our evacuation plans now."

"Not necessarily," Kira told him. "Quark's brother is on the job. And so is Odo, our chief of security."

Obahr eyed her. "Your chief of security is dealing with a Retizian? And that's going to get us our power coils?" He looked skeptical. "I must confess, I don't get it."

The major smiled. "It's a little complicated, I know. But our security chief is a shapeshifter."

Her friend raised an eyebrow. "You're joking, right? Aren't the shapeshifters the ones we're supposed to be looking out for?"

"A *friendly* shapeshifter," she added. "In any case, he's made himself up to look like Quark, so we would still have a shot at acquiring those power coils. That's why I wouldn't start making evacuation plans just yet."

Obahr turned away as he absorbed the information. Finally he looked back at her. "You think he can pull it off, this shapeshifter of yours?"

Kira shrugged. "I'm not certain even Quark himself could have pulled it off. But Odo has done the impossible before, Obahr. I'm just hoping he can do it again."

The administrator frowned. "So am I, Nerys. Pernon out."

As his image faded from her monitor, the major sighed—and wished she were as confident in Odo as she'd led Obahr to believe. If this were a firefight, there was no one she would rather have had at her side than the constable—even if he didn't use firearms personally.

But when it came to negotiating a business deal, Odo was out of his element, and Rom wasn't much of an insurance policy. And from what she understood,

Fel Jangor was as crafty as they came. In fact, the more Kira thought about it, the more pessimistic she became.

Abruptly her communicator badge emitted a beep. Tapping it, the major said: "Kira here."

"It's Julian," came the reply. "Major, I'm having some trouble with Quark. He seems to have disappeared."

Disappeared? The notion was almost comical. "Do you have any idea where he's gone?" the major asked.

"I do indeed," said the doctor. "According to the station's computer, he's at his bar—probably trying to open it for business."

She grunted. "That sounds about right. I'll take care of it immediately, Julian. Kira out."

Securing her station, she made her way across Ops. With Captain Sisko and Odo both absent from *Deep Space Nine,* she had to play security chief as well as commanding officer.

Fortunately it was only Quark she had to deal with, and a sick Quark at that. Barring any unforeseen circumstances, she'd have him back in the infirmary in a matter of minutes.

Barnes didn't say much on the way to her quarters. She couldn't. She was too beleaguered by the terrors of her imagination, despite the presence of Captain Sisko right beside her.

Alarms sounded in her mind, over and over again, jolting her each time. Flames rose and flickered behind her eyes. The ship seemed to lurch and come apart at the seams, and the ghosts of the dying reached out to her.

But she managed to keep her companion from knowing what was happening to her. After all, she had gotten good at covering up her madness. She had gotten *very* good.

Finally they reached her quarters. Forging ahead of the captain, Barnes tapped the padd beside the entrance. The doors opened and she entered, relieved to be able finally to sit down.

As she plunked herself on her bed, she breathed a sigh of relief. But Sisko wouldn't know what it was for, she told herself. He would think she was simply enervated by her experience on the bridge.

And embarrassed, of course. That would be only a natural reaction after the scene she had made, and the things she had said to Lieutenant Dax.

The captain regarded her for a moment, giving her a chance to settle herself. Then he folded his arms across his chest.

"All right," Sisko said. "Do you want to tell me what the hell went on out there, Counselor?"

Barnes looked up at him. She had waited a long time for this moment. But now that it was finally here, she found herself daunted by it, afraid to do what she had set out to do.

"I told you," she said softly, in answer to his question. "I just lost it, is all."

Even as Barnes uttered the words, she hated herself

for doing so. What was the matter with her, anyway? Why couldn't she do the thing that would finally set her free?

The captain shook his head. "No, Counselor. You're a professional—and by all accounts, a very accomplished professional. Sure, we're in a tough spot, but you're trained to deal with that." He paused. "There's more to it. There's got to be."

Barnes considered Sisko for a moment. Clearly the man was more perceptive than she had given him credit for. He had already seen deeper into the heart of her problem than Captain Kyprios ever could have.

Sighing, the counselor looked down at her hands. She had to tell him the truth, she thought, no matter what came of it. If he had come this far, he wouldn't stop until she emptied her heart to him.

Besides, that was what she wanted to do. What she *needed* to do. "You're right," she told him.

Barnes was intensely aware of her breathing, the pumping of her blood, the feeling of Sisko's eyes on her. And why not? This was conceivably the biggest moment of her life.

"There *is* more to it." She took a moment to lick her lips. "I know I shouldn't feel this way, but . . . I can't help seeing the destruction of the *Saratoga*. Over and over again."

Sisko recoiled a little. "The *Saratoga?*"

The counselor nodded. "Yes." There—she had taken the first step. It had to be easier from here on in.

The captain's eyes screwed tight. "But that was a

different situation entirely. We were under attack, facing a hostile force. And there were all those civilians on board . . ."

Her optimism faded. It might not be so easy after all.

"Of course it's different. I didn't mean to imply otherwise." The counselor leaned forward. "Please understand, what I'm feeling—"

"O'Brien to Captain Sisko." The chief's voice was loud in Barnes' small, cramped quarters.

"Sisko here," said the captain, gazing apologetically at Barnes. "I'm in Counselor Barnes's quarters, Mr. O'Brien. What's up?"

"We're just about finished here, sir. We've replicated all the engine parts we could—and as luck would have it, that was nearly all of them. The others have been replaced with close equivalents."

Sisko grunted. "Do you think it'll work?"

"Only one way to know," the chief replied. "And that's to put them through their paces."

The captain smiled hopefully. "I'm heading up to the bridge now. Brace yourself. Sisko out."

The counselor looked at him beseechingly. This had been her chance to escape her demons, at long last— her chance to be free. And suddenly it was slipping away from her.

"Don't go," she begged.

"We'll talk later," the captain promised her. "For now, we're wanted up on the bridge."

Barnes looked into his eyes. Was that mistrust she

saw there—brought on by her confession, or at least, the beginnings of it? Had she for once given away a hint of her madness?

No, she thought. Not mistrust. Just urgency, born of what O'Brien had told them. Just the call of duty.

Still there was time to finish what she had begun. Time to say what she needed to say. "But there's more," she insisted. "I need to—"

"Counselor," he said, this time in a noticeably sterner voice, "there's a lot at stake. We've got to go now." His eyes were hard and unyielding, the eyes of a man who was already somewhere else in spirit.

Barnes bit her lip. The opportunity was gone, she told herself. She could only hope there would be another one somewhere down the line.

But the line might not be very long. And while she wasn't afraid of dying per se, she was very much afraid of dying before she had liberated herself from her burden.

"All right," she told him. "I'm coming."

Reluctantly she got up from her bunk and followed Sisko to the bridge.

Kira found Quark just where the computer had placed him—at his bar. He was standing on the Promenade, announcing in a loud, ingratiating voice that the place was open for business.

Well, the major thought, she would have to put a stop to this. As she approached Quark, he caught a glimpse of her.

In that moment the battle lines were drawn.

By the look in his eyes, Kira could tell the Ferengi was going to do everything in his power to stay out of the infirmary. But as the Law around here, at least until Odo came back, the major was going to do everything she could to bring him back there.

"Please," Quark bellowed, opening his arms wide to the stream of passersby, "come on in—everyone! Sample the wares of the best entertainment establishment in three star systems!"

"I thought the place was closed," a corpulent Bajoran merchant called out. "Something about not paying your rent . . ."

"I pay my rent religiously," the Ferengi retorted, though in fact Captain Sisko hadn't asked him for any since he had arrived a few years ago. "We were closed only temporarily." He smiled, showing an abundance of teeth. "For . . . er, renovations, so we at Quark's Place can lavish our patrons with even more luxury than before."

The merchant peered past the Ferengi at the bar and its environs. "Doesn't look any different to *me*," he noted. "Just what did you renovate, Quark—your price list?"

There was a great deal of laughter in response. The Ferengi waved it away. "For your information," Quark said, "our holosuites have been upgraded to the state of the art and then some. Of course, it's not possible to tell that from the outside, but—"

Kira laid a hand on his shoulder and bent down to whisper in his ear. "Give it up," she told him.

The Ferengi turned to her with a scowl on his face. "You're keeping me from my livelihood, Major. Every minute my bar is closed is a tremendous loss of potential profits—and worse than that. If I don't get my clientele back immediately, someone else will."

Kira looked at him askance. "Quark, there *are* no other bars on the Promenade. Who do you think you're going to lose customers to—the Klingon eatery? Not everyone can stomach heart of *targ,* you know."

"That's not the point," the Ferengi insisted, "and I really don't have time to explain it to you. Now if you don't mind, Major, I'm in the process of attracting some business."

Quark made his way around Kira to continue his spiel. But by then, whatever crowd he had gathered had petered out. And despite the bar's obvious openness, there was still no one inside.

The Ferengi looked up at her. "You see what I mean, Major? Close your doors for a day or two and people forget you exist."

Kira shook her head. "If you don't get back to the infirmary, we're liable to forget *you* exist—and with good reason. Now—"

Quark frowned and held a hand up. "Hold on, Major. Let's talk this over." He tilted his head to indicate the bar. "Inside. Over a nice Bajoran wine, perhaps." The Ferengi snapped his fingers. "Something from Ducrain Province, I think. We've been getting some excellent wines from that region."

Kira smiled warily. "It's me, Quark—remember?

Do you think I'm dumb enough to let you get me drunk? Or to forget why I came here?"

The Ferengi regarded her with a sincerity she had never seen in him before. Either his acting had improved or he was pretty serious about something.

"All right," he told her. "No wine. Just a raktajino, if that's what you prefer. And it's on the house."

The Bajoran's eyes narrowed. Now she *knew* Quark was acting strangely. "Fine," she said. "A raktajino. But only for a few minutes."

"That's entirely up to you," the Ferengi replied reasonably.

Still leery of what Quark might be up to, Kira followed him into the bar and took a seat on one of the stools. As he had promised, the Ferengi made her a raktajino and set it before her. Then he came around the bar and climbed up on the stool beside her.

For a moment Quark didn't say anything. He seemed to be gathering his thoughts, putting his argument in order. Finally he spoke.

"Let me present you with a hypothetical case," the Ferengi began. "What would you do if Captain Sisko gave you a job to perform—an important job, mind you—and you came down with a little virus? Would you report to the infirmary? Or would you continue to discharge the responsibility the captain had given to you?"

The major frowned. "I see where you're going with this, Quark—but it's different. In one case, the welfare of the station could be at stake. And in the other case, all we're talking about is—"

"—is a bar," he said. "At least, in your estimation. But to a Ferengi, it's a place of business. And that makes it every bit as important, every bit as *holy,* as . . . well, as that temple you Bajorans have got on the Promenade."

Kira smiled. "That temple is a place of worship."

Quark leaned forward and tapped his forefinger on the bar. "So's this place, Major. *I* worship it. And so would any other Ferengi who derived profits from it. Just because you don't see it that way, don't denigrate *me* for doing so." He straightened on his stool. "And in return, I won't denigrate you for what *you* believe in."

Kira considered Quark's argument. She had to admit, he had a point. As much as she professed a tolerance for other races, a respect for what they held dear, it was easy to dismiss Ferengi behavior as something petty and reprehensible.

And maybe it *was*. But it was also the way their culture operated. And like any culture, it had a right to value whatever it liked, as long as no one else was hurt by it.

"I see what you're saying," she conceded. "I have to admit, I don't understand it, but I respect it." She sighed. "Unfortunately it doesn't change anything. I still have to take you back to the infirmary."

Quark held his hands out to her. "Why? Because that quack of a doctor says you do?"

The Bajoran nodded. "That quack of a doctor, as you put it, has the last word around here. Those are the rules on every Federation facility from Earth to the Romulan Neutral Zone."

"But I feel fine," the Ferengi insisted.

"That may be," said Kira, "but I've still got to take you back with me."

"Because of the *rules,*" he spat, his voice dripping with disdain.

"Because of the rules," she confirmed.

"And what about my sacred beliefs? My cultural imperative?" Quark bit his lip. "Look," he told her, holding out his fists in an appeal for understanding, "when you needed help getting those power coils, I was willing to lend a hand. Not eager, I'll admit, not thrilled about it—but I was still willing to help."

"Because I threatened you," she reminded him.

The Ferengi shook his head. "I would've done it anyway. I was just trying to see what kind of deal I could cut first."

Kira considered him for a moment—and found to her surprise that she believed him. "What are you saying?" she asked. "That because you were willing to help me with my problem, I should help you with yours?"

Quark shrugged. "I'm not endangering anyone else, Major. Only myself. And I doubt I'm doing even that. The only reason Dr. Bashir insists on keeping me in his torture chamber is because he doesn't grasp my cultural orientation." He paused. "At least, not the way you do."

The Bajoran leaned back in her chair. For a while she didn't say anything. She just tried to put herself in the Ferengi's shoes—to imagine what he was going through.

Suddenly, out of the corner of her eye, Kira caught sight of someone standing forlornly outside the bar. And she got an idea.

"All right," she told him. "You want to keep your bar open? Fine."

Quark grinned in a way that bordered on affection. "Really?" he said.

She nodded. "Really. The only catch is, you'll have to let someone else run the place—because you're going to the infirmary."

The Ferengi's expression became a pained one. "Someone else? But . . . but that's crazy. Who knows this bar the way I do?"

The major tilted her head to indicate the figure waiting outside the bar. *"He* does."

Following her gesture, Quark saw whom she was referring to. "Morn?" he replied. "You must be joking. He'll drink up all the profits."

"Then make it Nog," she suggested. "Or anyone else who'll agree to tend bar in your absence. That is," she remarked archly, "if keeping this place open is as vitally important as you say it is."

The Ferengi regarded her sourly. "I *thought* we had an understanding."

"Well," said Kira, smiling magnanimously, "I would say we do now."

Raising her raktajino to her lips, she drained her mug. Then she jerked a thumb in the direction of the exit.

"Shall we?"

Grumbling the whole time, Quark locked up the bar again and allowed her to escort him to the infirmary. En route, the Bajoran had a pang of guilt over the way she'd put the Ferengi in his place. Not a big one, but a pang nonetheless.

After all, there had been some sense to his argument. He really *was* a product of his culture.

Then she thought about all the bills Quark had padded over the years, all the drinks he had watered down and all the Dabo games he had fixed—and suddenly she didn't feel *that* bad.

CHAPTER
13

SISKO WOULD HAVE liked to stay in Barnes's quarters and hear the rest of what was on her mind. Unfortunately there were other matters at hand—and as the captain of the *Defiant*, he had to put those matters first.

Emerging from the turbolift onto the bridge, Sisko saw that Dax was no longer alone there. Lopez was hovering over the tactical console. On seeing the captain, the science officer turned and smiled.

"I've got the sensors pretty much back to where they should be," he reported, not without a certain amount of pride.

Sisko regarded him. "Good work, Lieutenant. You'll be pleased to hear O'Brien's team has made its repairs to the impulse engines." He turned to the Trill. "They're ready to try them out."

Dax nodded. "I'll take the helm."

As his friend crossed the bridge to the conn station, the captain looked up at the intercom grid hidden in the ceiling. After all, there was one member of the crew who hadn't been apprised of the latest development.

"Captain Sisko to Lieutenant Zar. We're about to restart the impulse engines. I thought you would want to know."

A moment later, the Bolian replied to the announcement. "Sickbay is secure, sir. And confident."

Sisko smiled. "Acknowledged, Mr. Zar. Chief O'Brien . . . you may begin reactivating the engines."

"Aye, sir," said O'Brien.

The captain eyed the viewscreen. The phenomenon was spawning cascade after cascade of color, mostly blues and yellows and purples. Sisko could almost imagine the thing staring back at him, confident in its power, daring the captain and his people to beat it.

"Here goes," O'Brien added.

At first nothing happened. Then Sisko felt a familiar vibration in the deck under his feet. It wasn't anything the captain would have noticed if he hadn't been concentrating on it—but he noticed it now.

Checking his console, he saw that there was activity in the impulse engines. What's more, it was steady activity, without any significant spikes up or down.

It was a good sign, he told himself. Of course, they still had quite a long way to go.

"They're up and running," O'Brien reported, just

for good measure. "And well within rated parameters."

"One-quarter impulse," Sisko said, glancing again at the gaudy display on the viewscreen. "On my mark. Engage."

He could feel the applied thrust. Again it was the sort of thing he might easily have overlooked if his attention had been drawn elsewhere, or if it had been the first time he had set foot on the *Defiant*.

But this was his ship. He knew it as well as he knew himself. And right now, his attention was right where it was supposed to be.

Dax looked up. "They're responding, Benjamin."

Lopez chuckled from his position at the tactical controls. "We're not falling into the nexus as quickly as we were before. Our descent has slowed by nearly thirty percent."

Out of the corner of his eye, the captain saw Barnes's face. The counselor seemed encouraged by what she had heard.

So far so good, he mused. But they would have to do better than that if they were to escape this thing.

"Up to half impulse," he ordered.

At the conn station, the Trill complied. The shudder in the deck plates got noticeably worse—and not just as a result of engine vibrations. The *Defiant* was feeling the stress of its struggle with the phenomenon.

"We've slowed again, sir," Lopez told them. "We're falling only half as fast as we were originally."

Sisko peered at the thing on the viewscreen. It was

mostly red now, spawning startling bursts of orange, pink, and powder blue. An endless symphony of color, but still deadly as a viper's nest. The captain couldn't let himself forget that.

"Full impulse, Dax."

This time Sisko didn't watch his officer make the necessary adjustments on her control padds. He didn't have to. A moment later, the whole ship began to shiver like a string in a Vulcan lyre.

But the engines seemed to be holding up fine. The captain turned to Lopez for a progress report.

The science officer instantly noticed the scrutiny. "We're fighting it to a standstill, sir. We're not making any headway, unfortunately—but at least we're not losing ground."

Sisko nodded. "All right, then. We seem to have bought ourselves some time. Now let's see if we can't capitalize on it." He glanced at Dax. "Lieutenant, try the—"

Without warning, the deck lurched savagely beneath him. Latching on to his armrest, he was able to remain on his feet—but Barnes, who had been standing next to him, went careening into the captain's side.

To keep the counselor from sprawling when the deck pitched again, he wrapped an arm around her midsection. But there was no "again." The ship seemed to have righted itself.

For a second or so, Sisko found himself staring into Barnes's face—into her deep, dark eyes, full of an anxiety he hadn't quite plumbed yet. There was something disturbing in those depths, no question about it. But there was also something eminently and undeniably appealing.

He was aware of the nearness of her, of her body pressed against his, perhaps more than he should have been. And he knew by her expression that the counselor was aware of it as well.

This isn't the time, the captain told himself. And even if it were, there was Kasidy to think about.

Flushing with embarrassment, Sisko disengaged himself from Barnes. Then, putting the incident behind him, he moved purposefully toward Dax.

"What happened?" he asked—though, of course, he already knew the answer.

The Trill sighed as she looked up at him. "The engines couldn't take the strain. They're not responding."

The captain cursed softly. "Mr. O'Brien," he called out. The bridge rang with his summons. "What's going on?"

The chief didn't sound happy as he replied. "Apparently a couple of the replacement parts didn't have the integrity of the originals. They cracked under the strain—and we're out of replicator material. Looks like we're back to square one, sir."

And with a couple of hours' less time to do something about it. Sisko noted the disappointment of those around him.

"It was a good try," he told O'Brien. "You'll just have to come up with something else, Chief. Sisko out."

Barnes didn't say anything. Her mouth a tight line, she turned and headed back toward the turbolift.

"Counselor?" said the captain.

She stopped and looked back over her shoulder, her eyes still as deep and dark and mysterious as ever. "Sir?"

"Are you all right?" he asked her.

After a moment, Barnes nodded. "I'm fine. I think you were right—I just need some rest." Then she entered the lift and the doors closed behind her.

Sisko regarded the turbolift. Apparently the counselor wasn't quite so eager to unburden herself as she had been before. Just as well, he thought—though he was curious as to what she would have said.

Swinging himself into the center seat, he looked at Dax and then Lopez. The science officer was trying to hide his frustration, though he wasn't doing a very good job of it. And Dax? After living so many lives in so many different bodies, she had learned to keep her thoughts to herself.

Resting his elbows on his armrests, Sisko made a steeple of his fingers and confronted the viewscreen anew. The colors of the wave nexus twisted and broke like a rainbow surf on invisible rocks. Blues and yellows folded into one another and emerged as streamers of orange-red.

Chaos. Utter chaos. The kind one encountered only in nightmares, where the rules were suspended and the unconscious took over.

But this was no dream. It was as real as life and death, and it was dragging them deeper into itself by the minute. If there was a way out, it seemed to say, the captain and his people would have to find it soon—or suffer the horrific consequences.

As Odo and Rom entered Fel Jangor's parlor again, their host smiled at Odo from his wooden chair. The shapeshifter smiled back as best he could. After all, that was the hardest expression for him to emulate.

"I trust you had a good night's sleep," said Jangor.

"Excellent," replied Odo.

"Most wonderful," effused the Ferengi.

"And an ample first meal?"

"Quite satisfying," said the constable.

"And tasty," Rom added.

"Good," their host responded. "Then we can resume our negotiations immediately."

"I would like that," Odo told him.

Reluctantly he settled into the long, dark couch. As before, his feet dangled over the front of it. It was still a humiliating feeling, but he did his best to put it aside.

"As I see it," the changeling began, "this is really a very simple matter. You have the power coils. I want them."

The Retizian's eyes narrowed with interest. "Go on."

"Now," Odo continued, "you and I could dance around the subject for hours if we wished, wheeling out every bargaining tactic in our considerable arsenals—and they *are* considerable, I think you'll agree."

"Without reservation," Jangor conceded.

"Or," said the shapeshifter, "we could come right to the point. I am prepared to pay you seven bars of gold-pressed latinum apiece. That's seventy bars for all ten. And I hope you will not be offended when I say this is my final offer."

Rom sat in his seat, saying nothing. He hadn't been at all comfortable with this approach back in their quarters, but eventually he had agreed to it—knowing he really had no other choice.

The Retizian chuckled. "There's no such thing as a final offer, Quark. We both know that."

Odo shook his head slowly from side to side. "Normally, that would be true. It would merely be a starting point. But not in this case, my friend. Seventy bars, take it or leave it."

Jangor looked at him. Then he tilted his head and looked at him from a fresh perspective. "You're joking," he concluded.

"No joke," the constable assured him.

The Retizian's mottled skin turned darker, except for the mottles. Odo recognized it as a sign of wariness. For all he knew, Jangor would get up and walk out of the parlor, insulted by the severity of the offer.

But Jangor didn't get up. Slowly, very slowly, a smile spread across his face. He stroked the black quills protruding from his chin.

"Very clever," he mused out loud. "I should have known I couldn't put one over on *you*, Quark."

Put one over . . . ? Odo did his best not to make his

surprise manifest. "Why, whatever do you mean?" he asked innocently.

"You're not insulted?" the Retizian asked.

"Of course not," remarked the constable. He still had no idea what they were talking about. "Business is business, even among friends."

Jangor grinned. "I've often said so myself. But tell me, how did you find out I was having trouble peddling the power coils?"

Ah, thought Odo. So that was it. "Word has a way of getting around."

The Retizian sighed. "So it does."

"Then you'll accept our offer?" Rom blurted, barely able to control himself.

Jangor looked at him. "I thought I already had," he noted.

"Though not in so many words," Odo observed, more for the Ferengi's benefit than that of their host. "We can work out the delivery details later, of course."

"Of course," said Jangor. He tilted his head to the other side. "You know, Quark, you've changed."

"I have?" asked the shapeshifter, a little nervously.

"Indeed," the Retizian replied. "The old Quark would never have made a take-it-or-leave-it proposition, no matter how many cards he held in his hand."

Odo shrugged. "It seemed like the right thing to do at the time."

"Actually," Jangor told him, "I *like* the change. At my age, I don't have time for bobbing and weaving.

I've come to prefer the straightforward to the circumspect."

"In that case," said the changeling, with unqualified sincerity, "I'm glad to have been of service."

The Retizian's eyes narrowed. "Of course, if your price hadn't been what I had in mind to begin with, I would still have turned it down—straightforward or not."

Odo smiled at Jangor, despite the difficulty of doing so. "Of course," he replied. "That's why you're a legend in this sector. No one pulls the wool over your eyes."

The Retizian looked at him. "The wool . . . ?"

"It's just an expression," the shapeshifter assured him. "It comes from spending too much time in the company of humans."

Jangor grimaced as if he were in pain. "Humans. Eucch. They make my quills stand on end."

"Mine, too," Rom responded. "That is, they would if I had them." He paused. "Quills, I mean—not humans." Another pause. "That didn't come out the way I intended. What I was *trying* to say—"

Odo slid forward off the couch, concerned that Quark's brother would yet find a way to wreck the deal. "I'm afraid we must be going now, my friend. I have a bar to see to, as you know. But I hope we'll be able to do business again sometime."

The Retizian nodded. "Yes, Quark. And soon." He squinted mischievously. "Perhaps I'll even pay you a visit on that station of yours."

The changeling eyed him. "Aren't you worried that

our constable will nab you? You are a wanted man, you know."

Jangor dismissed the idea with a wave of his hand. "The lawman hasn't been invented who can keep up with the likes of Fel Jangor."

Odo smiled again. Somehow, it was less difficult this time. "In that case," he said, "I look forward to seeing you there."

CHAPTER
14

IN ENGINEERING, THE mood was a decidedly somber one. But then, failure had a way of putting a damper on things, especially when people's lives were on the line. And in the half hour or so since that failure, neither Chief O'Brien nor either of his two colleagues had come up with anything even resembling a usable suggestion.

O'Brien watched Lieutenant Commander Graal pace from one end of the room to the other. For a Craynid, it was a very long, slow trip.

Thorn, on the other hand, barely moved. He just sat there in his chair, his tiny blue eyes squinting as he pondered the problem.

The chief couldn't take the silence. "There's another way out of this soup," he insisted. "It's just a question of finding it."

The bearded man nodded. "And if we can't, who can? I mean, are we or are we not some of the best minds in Starfleet?"

O'Brien looked at him. "Damned right we are. And it's not the first time we've been in a jam, either."

"You're not kidding," Thorn agreed. "I can think of a dozen worse scrapes—and that's just since I left the *Saratoga*. Or to be more accurate, since the *Saratoga* left all of us."

"The point," said O'Brien, "is this shouldn't be that hard. We should have had a brainstorm by now. We should have had this thing licked."

Suddenly the Craynid stopped pacing. Turning to the two humans, she spoke in her strange, whistling voice. "I have an idea," she said.

The bearded man breathed a sigh of relief. "Well, let's hear it, Commander. It's got to be better than what we've come up with so far."

O'Brien grunted. "By all means."

Graal looked at him, seemingly oblivious to the humans' sarcasm. "The *Defiant* has several probes, correct?"

"That it does," O'Brien told her. "Seven of them, to be exact. And all in good shape, from what I could tell."

"That is good," she replied.

"What did you intend to do with them?" asked Thorn.

The Craynid shrugged. "Shoot them out of the nexus."

O'Brien regarded her. "What for?"

Graal blinked a few times. "If we shot them out, we could use our tractor beams to latch on to them."

The chief saw what she meant now. "You're saying we could hitch a ride on them. Use them to haul ourselves to safety."

The Craynid nodded. "Precisely."

O'Brien and Thorn looked at each other, pondering the possibilities. Graal had something there, all right. They both knew it.

The big man turned to her, trying to contain his enthusiasm and doing a bad job of it. "But can a bunch of these probes haul a mass like the *Defiant*'s? That's no mean feat."

O'Brien did some quick computations. "Possibly," he said at last. He rubbed his chin. "Of course, there's a way to find out for certain. We can run a computer simulation of the commander's plan."

"But that'll cost us precious time," argued Thorn. "Why not just try it in the real world, before we get pulled any deeper into the nexus?"

Certainly that would maximize their chances for success, O'Brien conceded. Nonetheless, it was his duty to advise caution.

"We can't waste the probes," he decided. "They may turn out to be useful to us in some other way."

The big man shook his head. "With all due respect, Chief, we haven't got much time left. What in blazes are we saving them for?"

O'Brien shrugged. "One never knows. And since there's still enough time to run a simulation, I say we do it." He turned to Graal for a tiebreaker. "What do you think, Commander?"

The Craynid stared at him with those round black eyes of hers. "I prefer to run a simulation," she replied.

"There we go," said O'Brien. "And since it's your idea, would you care to set it up?"

"As you wish," Graal responded.

Rising, she moved to the computer table and went to work. O'Brien and Thorn went with her. After all, they had something of a stake in whatever she found out.

The changeling sat back in his plush seat and eyed the pentagonal viewscreen across the room. On it, he could see Fel Jangor's ship slowly receding from view.

Actually, the Retizian's vessel wasn't moving at all. It was the ship carrying Odo and Rom—the one they had hired to transport them from *Deep Space Nine* and then back again—that was withdrawing from the rendezvous coordinates.

The shapeshifter couldn't help but feel a certain satisfaction with what he had accomplished. Despite his misgivings, despite the shame that had accompanied his transformation, he had triumphed.

More important, Odo had performed a valuable service. Kira's friend on Bajor would have the power coils he required. His city would be protected from floods for another decade at least.

That is, unless something *else* went wrong with the water pumps. And if they did, that would be someone else's problem.

In short, things could have turned out a lot worse. And that, as Quark himself might have said, was the bottom line.

Abruptly Rom entered the room. As on the trip out, he had loaded a large tray with replicated delicacies and was all but drooling at the prospect of consuming them.

The constable shook his head. *Food.* Outside of its being a biological necessity, he had never understood the attraction it held—nor why someone as small as a Ferengi would wish to ingest such prodigious quantities of it. But then, he concluded with uncharacteristic generosity, to each his own.

Rom looked at him. "What's so funny?" he asked.

Odo returned the look. "Funny? What do you mean?"

"You're smiling," the Ferengi observed. "Of course, I'd be smiling too, if I'd consummated such a profitable deal."

The shapeshifter glanced at the reflective surface on one of the bulkheads. Rom hadn't lied. He really *was* smiling—and with Quark's face.

Strange, he thought, how a leer made him look even more like the Ferengi than before. Shuddering, he eliminated it.

Bad enough he was forced to maintain Quark's appearance until they returned to *Deep Space Nine;* resembling the bar owner *too* much was an unnecessary source of discomfort.

Rom thrust the tray full of delicacies at him. "Would you like one? I can always get more."

Odo shook his head. "No. Thank you. I don't eat."

The Ferengi looked disappointed. "That's right," he said. "You don't, do you?" He shrugged. "Not that I really mind eating by myself. Quark makes me do it all the time."

The shapeshifter sighed. In the end, he supposed, Rom had been a less onerous companion than he had anticipated.

Certainly the Ferengi was inept in many respects, annoying at times, and occasionally even incomprehensible. But Rom had provided Odo with a valuable perspective. Without it the transaction with Fel Jangor would never have been completed for the desired sum.

"On second thought," said the constable, feigning an interest in the delicacies, "I believe I'll have something after all."

His companion looked at him. "I thought you didn't eat."

"I don't," Odo confirmed. "Not usually, that is. But once in a great while, I make an exception."

Rom beamed at him. "Excellent. Try one of the Flavanian beetle canapés. They're my favorites."

The changeling picked up one of the canapés and considered it more closely. Something inside it—presumably, a Flavanian beetle—was still wriggling.

The things I do for my friends, he thought.

As the door to sickbay slid aside, Sisko peered into the room. The lights had been turned down low.

"Zar?" he called softly.

The Bolian had pulled a chair up to Laffer's biobed and was sitting by her side. He acknowledged his friend's entrance with a glance.

"For a moment, I thought you were Barnes," he said soberly. "But she's not as tall as you are. And as I recall, she doesn't have a beard."

The captain shook his head, amazed at his friend's resilience. "Leave it to you to joke at a time like this."

Zar shrugged. "Some would say this is the best time for it."

Crossing sickbay, Sisko joined the Bolian at their colleague's bedside and made a quick survey of her readouts. "She's no better," he noted.

"But no worse," Zar pointed out. "On the other hand, it may not matter in a few hours."

"Pessimism?" Sisko gibed. "From *you*? The man who pulled our bacon out of the fire at Guldammur Four?"

"Let's call it realism," the Bolian suggested. "Unless we're really barreling our way out of here and no one's bothered to tell me."

The captain put a hand on his friend's shoulder. "I wouldn't do that to you, Zar. But on the other hand,

I'm not ready to give up, either. O'Brien and Graal are two of the best engineers in the business—and Thorn's as resourceful as they come. I still have faith in their abilities."

The Bolian grunted. "I only wish Graal didn't need so much time to ponder a problem." A smile spread across his face. "Remember that time in the lounge, when Captain Saros tried to teach her to play chess?"

As the memory came to the surface, Sisko laughed. "Yes," he said, "as a matter of fact I do. She took half an hour to move her first pawn."

Zar looked up at him. "Then, halfway through the captain's second move, she wanted to take her first one back. And for the life of her, she couldn't understand why he wouldn't allow it."

Sisko nodded. "The captain didn't want to lose his patience with her—especially in front of the whole crew. But even a steadfast Vulcan like Saros had to be getting a little testy. It's a good thing that priority message came through from Starfleet Command, or he might have been stuck there with her for hours."

The Bolian's eyes narrowed. "You're kidding me, right?"

"About what?" the captain asked.

"About Starfleet Command. I just made that message up."

Sisko looked at him. "You *what?*"

Zar grinned. "I made it up. I saw the captain squirming, so I went up to the bridge and commandeered the tactical console. Then I summoned him to his quarters for an eyes-only communique from Admiral Quinn."

"But Quinn never sent it?" Sisko was stunned. "And you never told me about this?"

"I thought I had," the Bolian responded sheepishly. "I guess I never got around to it."

"Remind me to put you on report." The captain harrumphed. "Impersonating an admiral is a court-martial offense."

"So it is," Zar countered. "You can bring me up on charges if we get back." He turned a darker shade of blue. "I mean *when* we get back. A little slip of the tongue, I guess."

For a moment, there was an uncomfortable silence, as the reality of their situation intruded on the conversation. Then Sisko recalled another incident, only a bit more recent than the first.

"Mariphasa Four," he said.

The Bolian smiled. "That run-in we had with the Cardassians, where they captured our away team?"

The captain looked at his fallen colleague, her skin pallid and clammy-looking. He nodded. "You and me and the doctor here, facing the prospect of torture if we didn't reveal the nature of our mission."

Zar chuckled. "And Laffer got into an argument with the Cardassian commander over what effect their weapons would have on us. He said it would take him over a minute to fry us to death—"

"—and she insisted it would take a lot less." Sisko shook his head, finding it hard to believe even now.

"Something about Cardassians shedding heat more efficiently than humans or Bolians."

"And she wouldn't back down," the lieutenant recalled, "not even when he threatened to make a test case out of her. Of course, as it turned out, her stubbornness was a good thing."

"Uh-huh." The captain looked at his friend. "It gave you a chance to disarm one of the other Cardassians, and turn the tables on them."

Zar looked at him a little dubiously. "I thought it was *you* who disarmed that Cardassian."

Sisko thought about it, then shook his head. "No, I'm pretty sure it was you. Unless—" Suddenly he remembered. "Thorn."

The Bolian threw his hands up. "Of course. There were *four* of us in that landing party originally. But Thorn separated from us for some reason."

"Still," said the captain, "regardless of who made the move, it was Laffer who bought us the time we needed."

As before, there was a moment of wistful silence. This time, it was Zar who ended it. "Thetalian Prime," he declared.

Sisko knew just what he was talking about. "The doctor's just saved the crew from an epidemic of alien organisms. You and I wake up in sickbay, hungry as wolves."

"We demand something to eat," the Bolian remembered. "And Laffer tells us we're not really hungry— we're thirsty."

The captain couldn't help but laugh. "I say I can tell

the difference between hunger and thirst, and she argues with me."

"And me, too," said Zar, laughing along with him. "But the worst part—" He began laughing even harder. "The worst part—"

Suddenly, Sisko was giggling so hard he couldn't speak. Hell, he could hardly breathe. He bit his lip, but it didn't help.

Zar was out of control, too, by then, shaking in the grip of it and not caring a bit. Tears began to roll down his pale blue cheeks.

Maybe it was the strain of what had happened to them here on the *Defiant,* or the incredible absurdity of the memory, or a little of both. It didn't matter, the captain thought. It felt good—damned good.

Clamping a hand on his friend's shoulder, he tried to speak—but he couldn't. All he could do was sputter.

"The worst part," Zar finally squeezed out, "was that she was right. We weren't hungry after all."

"That's right," the captain confirmed through clenched teeth. "That bug we picked up had mangled the connections in our brains. What we thought was hunger—"

"—was actually thirst!" the lieutenant finished.

And they laughed some more, long and heartily, until sickbay echoed with the sound of it and their faces were streaked with tears. Finally it subsided, and they took a couple of deep breaths.

"Oh my," said Sisko. "Oh my, oh my."

"We've got to do this more often," Zar noted. He

wiped away some tears. "Though not necessarily under these circumstances."

"I know what you mean," the captain agreed. He looked at Laffer again, feeling her plight even more strongly than before. "You know," he said, "this woman used to irritate me something fierce. But I would give anything to see her get up from that bed and do it again."

The Bolian smiled sadly. "I'm no doctor," he replied, "but I wouldn't hope too hard. We've only got a few hours left, and I doubt she'll regain consciousness in that time. But then, maybe she's luckier than we are."

Sisko looked at him. "What do you mean?"

Zar shrugged. "Odds are we're all going to die here, Captain. The only difference is, Laffer isn't worried about it."

Abruptly an intercom voice flooded the room. "O'Brien to Sisko."

"Sisko here," said the captain. He looked up at the intercom grid. "Tell me you've got something, Chief."

O'Brien hesitated. Sisko knew the news wasn't going to be what the crew was hoping for.

"Sorry, sir. We're done with our computer simulation of the probe-and-tractor-beam approach—and it didn't work. The probes' engines burned out before they could pull us free."

The captain sighed. "I'd like to pat you on the back for all your hard work, Chief. Unfortunately we're running out of time. You've got to come up with something else, and quickly."

Again O'Brien hesitated. "Actually, sir, we already *have* come up with something else."

Sisko darted a glance at Zar. The Bolian shrugged. "What are you waiting for?" said the captain. "Fill me in."

O'Brien did as he was told. Before he had gotten very far, it was clear why the chief had hesitated.

"Not an easy plan to carry out," Zar observed.

"But it's an option," the captain reminded him. "And under the circumstances, it might be the only one we have."

CHAPTER
15

SISKO STOOD IN front of his center seat and considered his officers. They looked back at him with varying degrees of curiosity.

O'Brien, Graal, and Thorn knew what he was going to say, of course, since it was their efforts that had made the meeting necessary. And though Zar was still sequestered with Dr. Laffer in sickbay, he also knew what would be discussed, having heard about it when the captain did.

But Dax, Lopez, and Counselor Barnes looked at Sisko expectantly, having little or no idea what was going on. Of course, that deficit would be erased in the next couple of minutes.

The captain looked to the intercom grid in the ceiling. "Are you with us, Lieutenant Zar?"

"I'm here," the Bolian replied, as cheerful as ever. "You can get on with it anytime, sir."

Satisfied, Sisko eyed the others. "Our engineering team has come up with another strategy," he explained.

"That's good," Lopez commented dryly. "I was beginning to fear we'd be in this nexus forever."

The captain ignored the attempt at black humor. Turning to the head of his engineering team, he nodded. "Go ahead, Chief."

O'Brien took it from there. "Back when I was serving on the *Enterprise,*" he explained, "we received a Klingon emissary who had crossed vast stretches of space in nothing more than a specially equipped probe."

Barnes looked at him. "A probe? Really?"

The engineer nodded. "Her name was K'Ehleyr. And she had a lot of guts, let me tell you—Klingon probes aren't built nearly as well as ours are. Which brings me to my point." He looked around. "With the help of Lieutenant Commander Graal and Mr. Thorn here, I believe I can equip the *Defiant*'s probes for humanoid occupation. That is, we can use them to get us out of here."

Lopez grunted. "Brilliant idea, Chief."

O'Brien frowned. "There's only one problem with it."

Sisko already knew what the problem was, but he let his people figure it out for themselves. Finally Dax said it out loud.

"There are only seven probes," she pointed out.

"And according to my calculations . . . there are nine of us."

"That's right," the chief confirmed grimly. "Which means two of us will have to stay behind on the *Defiant.*"

Where they would face certain death. As the captain looked around, he could see no one had missed that little detail.

O'Brien took a deep breath. "Since it's my idea, I volunteer to be one of the two who stay behind."

Sisko shook his head. "You shouldn't be penalized for not being able to save everyone, Chief. Besides, you've got a wife and daughter."

"And you've got a son," O'Brien countered.

"He's right," Zar remarked over the intercom system. "Think about Jake, sir. He still needs you."

"He's not a baby anymore," the captain declared for the Bolian's benefit. "Not like Molly. He can learn to live without me."

"This is all quite irrelevant," the Craynid whistled. "I have no less than one hundred and thirty offspring—a healthy brood even by *my* people's standards. Yet I would stay if it meant others might survive."

Sisko had never thought of Graal as particularly courageous. But then, maybe he hadn't known her as well as he thought.

"I hate to be the one to point this out," said Thorn, "but Dr. Laffer probably won't survive a journey in a jury-rigged probe. As far as I can tell, there's no point in saving one for her."

"We don't know that," Barnes replied.

"Yes, we do," he insisted. "And since I've got no real ties to anyone, I'll stay here with her."

The captain scrutinized the security chief. Interesting behavior for a man who'd been accused of sabotaging the ship.

But in the end, he shook his head. "No," he told Thorn. "There's no fair way to determine who stays and who goes."

"But we can't *all* stay," Lopez reminded them.

Sisko turned to him. "Then we draw straws."

Dax's brow wrinkled. "Straws, Benjamin?"

"Figuratively speaking," the captain amended. He looked to the viewscreen. "Computer, place eight Federation symbols on the main viewer. Then hide a small representation of the *Defiant* behind one of them. I leave it up to you to decide which one."

"Acknowledged," the computer responded.

A moment later the Federation symbols appeared. As Sisko had requested, there were eight of them.

"Hang on a minute," said Lopez. "There are *nine* of us."

Sisko nodded. "That's right. I'm invoking the captain's privilege—some would say responsibility—to go down with his ship."

"But, sir—" O'Brien began.

Sisko silenced him with a glare. "I'm not inviting any further discussion on the point. Case closed, Chief."

Reluctantly O'Brien shut up. In fact, they all did.

The captain pulled down on the front of his tunic.

"All right, then. Whoever picks the symbol with the *Defiant* behind it stays. The rest take the probes. Understand?"

Zar said he did. Everyone else just nodded.

"I'll go first," Thorn told them. He faced the screen, where the eight symbols were hovering in three tiers against the wildly beautiful background of the nexus. "Computer," he said, "show me what's behind the symbol in the center."

A moment later, the symbol disappeared. There was nothing behind it but empty space.

"What happened?" asked Zar.

Thorn told him. They could all hear the sound of relief in the big man's voice, no matter how much he would have denied it.

Next, it was O'Brien's turn. "Give me the symbol in the upper-right-hand corner," he said.

There was nothing behind that one either.

Dax went after him. Then Graal. Neither of them drew the dreaded "short straw."

That left Lopez, Laffer, Zar, and Barnes. The tension in the air was almost palpable. It throbbed in Sisko's temples.

Lopez gestured for Barnes to go ahead of him. "Please," he said gallantly.

But the counselor shook her head. "No," she told him. "Go ahead. I'll go last."

The science officer turned to the screen. "Very well," he muttered. Then he spoke in a louder voice. "Computer, I'll take the bottom tier, in the center."

The response was instantaneous. The Starfleet symbol vanished—leaving nothing in its wake. Lopez glanced at Barnes, then the captain.

"I guess we should give Zar his shot now," he suggested.

Noting the counselor's preference, Sisko nodded. "Ready, Zar?"

"Ready," the Bolian confirmed. "Has anyone taken the middle tier, on the left?"

"Not yet," the captain informed him. "Is that what you want?"

A beat. "Yes," said Zar. "That's the one."

Sisko looked up. "Computer, delete the symbol in the middle tier, on the left."

The computer complied. "Well?" asked the Bolian, who couldn't see what was going on. "Is it you and I, Captain?"

"No," said Sisko, his eyes on the viewscreen. "You'll be on one of those escape pods, Mr. Zar." He glanced at the counselor. "Your turn," he advised, as gently as possible. After all, Dr. Laffer could hardly choose for herself.

Barnes nodded, the muscles in her jaw fluttering. There were only two symbols left, both in the top row. One was in the center, the other to the left of it.

"The one in the middle," she announced, her voice surprisingly strong.

"Computer," said the captain, "delete the symbol in the top row, center."

The symbol disappeared—and revealed the tiny *Defiant* lurking behind it.

"My god," whispered Lopez.

But if the counselor was devastated by the result, she didn't show it. She just blinked a couple of times as someone informed Zar of the result.

Sisko felt a hand on his shoulder. Turning, he saw that it belonged to Chief O'Brien. The man's expression was one of great sincerity.

"Sir, I wish it had worked out differently," O'Brien told him.

The captain acknowledged the gesture. "Thanks, Chief. So do I."

He turned to his officers again. This time, it wasn't curiosity he saw on their faces. It was either pity or regret—or in Thorn's case, perhaps a combination of both.

Only Barnes showed no emotion. She was still looking at the viewscreen, seemingly unable to absorb the significance of what had happened. Sisko's heart went out to her, but he had orders to give.

"O'Brien, Graal, Thorn," said the captain. "I'll need you to outfit those probes for passenger transport. Dax and Lopez, download as much information as you can from the computer banks."

"Aye, sir," the Trill responded dutifully, only a thin strain of sentiment insinuating itself into her voice.

"Aye," Lopez chimed in.

"Counselor Barnes will remain with me on the bridge," Sisko announced. "Everyone else is dismissed."

CHAPTER
16

SISKO TURNED TO the freestanding control panel beside his seat and glanced again at the chronometer in the corner of it. According to the projections he'd gotten from Dax, they had less than an hour to go before the nexus pulled the *Defiant* apart.

For a long time, the ship had remained steadfast against the energies swirling around it, only a subtle tremor in the deck plates betraying its struggle. But that was no longer the case.

Now, despite her inertial dampers, the *Defiant* was pitching and rolling like an ancient schooner on Earth's whitecapped waters. And it was going to get worse, the captain knew. *Much* worse.

Tapping his communicator, Sisko established a link with O'Brien. "Chief, how much longer before the probes are ready?"

"Not much longer," O'Brien replied. "Just a few minutes, sir."

The captain scowled. "Keep me posted. Sisko out."

He surveyed the bridge. It was just he and Barnes, and the counselor was sitting at the Ops console. Sensing Sisko's scrutiny, she swiveled around to face him.

"I'm done," she told him. "I've initialized the launches. All you need to do is give the order."

He nodded. "Thanks, Counselor."

Barnes smiled a faint smile. "You're welcome, Captain."

He was reminded of the conversation they'd had in her quarters—the one they'd never finished. At the time, she had confessed that their plight recalled the *Saratoga*'s destruction for her.

Sisko hadn't quite seen the analogy—or maybe he hadn't wanted to see it. But he saw it now with painful clarity. The details weren't the same, but they didn't have to be. It was the sense of utter helplessness, of imminent death, that bound the two situations together.

He thought about saying something about it to the counselor now that fate had thrown them together— tying up the loose end, as it were. However, Barnes seemed to have gotten a grip on herself since then. Maybe it would be smarter not to bring it up.

O'Brien's voice interrupted the captain's reverie. "I believe we're ready, sir," he reported.

Sisko leaned back in his chair. "We're ready, too," he replied.

There was a pause on the other end. "Sir," said the chief, "there's a lot I'd like to say. And I'm not the only one."

The captain nodded. "I know, Mr. O'Brien. Unfortunately we don't have time for that sort of thing."

The engineer was stubborn, as Sisko knew he would be. "Begging your pardon, sir, but we're not likely to have another chance."

"I know that, too," the captain assured him.

He saw Barnes glance at him, as if to advise him that a moment or two wouldn't hurt. Sisko frowned.

"It's been an honor working with you, Chief. And you as well, Old Man, and Zar and Graal and Lopez and Thorn—the whole lot of you. And I know you feel the same way. Now it's time for you to tuck yourselves in, and to leave the rest to myself and Counselor Barnes—and that's all the good-bye you're going to get." He grunted. "Sisko out."

As if to underline the urgency of his directive, the ship lurched and shuddered violently. The shields wouldn't hold much longer under this kind of punishment. They would have to move ahead with their plan.

The captain turned to Barnes. "It's time," he told her. "If you don't mind, I'll execute the launches myself."

"Of course," she answered.

He thought he heard a tremor in her voice. A slight one, but a tremor nonetheless. Nor could he have blamed her for it, given the apparent hopelessness of their situation.

He leaned forward, the probes forgotten for the moment. "Counselor?"

Barnes didn't answer. She just sat there, her back turned to him as if she was merely intent on her control panel. Then, slowly, her head drooped onto her chest.

"Counselor?" he said again.

Her hands rose to cover her face. Still she made no sound, but it was clear she was caught in the grip of a powerful emotion. Before long, her shoulders were shaking with the force of it.

Apparently Barnes hadn't recovered from her fears after all—she had only submerged them for a while. Getting up out of his seat, Sisko approached the Ops station.

He wished the woman hadn't had to go through this. He wished there had been another way—but time was running down like sand in an hourglass, and another way hadn't presented itself.

"Counselor?" he said a third time, when he was standing right in back of her. "I know how hard this has got to be."

Barnes turned to look at him. Suddenly the captain realized he had been wrong about her. Dead wrong. The counselor's tears hadn't been caused by grief or terror. If they had been, she wouldn't have been smiling through them.

And there was no question she was smiling—with a transcendent joy that nudged him off balance. Sisko shook his head.

"I don't understand," he said simply.

"I'm not afraid," the counselor told him with a certain pride in her voice. "Not of dying, anyway."

The captain looked at her. "Then of what?"

The tears made her eyes look liquid and beautiful, like droplets of distilled darkness. "I was afraid," Barnes went on, "that I would die without ever telling you."

"Telling me?" he repeated. What was she talking about? Why was she being so mysterious all of a sudden? Unless . . .

. . . unless the counselor was the saboteur, and this was her confession.

Instinctively Sisko took a step back, wary of her. But she had no weapons in her hands, nothing with which she might hurt him.

Barnes got to her feet. "Yes," she replied, wiping away a tear. "Telling you. About my crime."

The captain's eyes narrowed. He had been right, apparently. The counselor was the one to blame for their predicament.

As Barnes came closer, he could feel himself recoiling inside—and not just because she had placed his friends and his vessel at risk. There was something strange about her, something unfocused.

Something a little insane, he thought. Yes, that was it. He wondered now why he hadn't seen it before.

"Please," she said, hands held palms out as she closed the gap between them. "Don't be afraid." Her eyes opened wide, pleading with him. "Can't you see, Benjamin? Can't you see . . . I'm in love with you?"

Sisko shook his head, genuinely surprised. "In love . . . ?" he echoed.

"Yes," the counselor confirmed. "In love, since the moment I first saw you on the *Saratoga.*" Her eyes glazed over as she revisited the memory. "You were tall, handsome, firm and gentle at the same time. Was it any wonder you took my breath away?"

The captain fought to regain his equilibrium. One puzzle at a time, for god sakes. "You said something about a crime," he reminded her.

A shadow fell over Barnes's face. "Yes," she said. "But I only did it for you, Benjamin."

"Did what?" Sisko insisted. "What did you *do* for me, Counselor?"

She looked away from him, as if distracted by something. Her features took on an almost childlike expression.

"I could have saved her," moaned Barnes. "I *could* have."

The captain was going to ask who the counselor was talking about. Laffer, maybe? But the doctor wasn't dead—at least not yet.

Then who? What "she" could Barnes have meant? And then, with stunning certainty, he *knew*.

"She was pinned under all that wreckage, half-crushed by it," the counselor continued. "But she was still alive. Still struggling. I could have gotten help, Benjamin."

My god, he thought. My god.

She looked up at Sisko, her eyes red-rimmed and

full of tears now. "Part of me wanted to. But another part thought if she were dead . . . if she were out of the picture . . ."

The captain felt as if he'd been hit with a sledge-hammer. His stomach tightening painfully, his senses reeling, he reached out for the nearest bulkhead to steady himself.

". . . if your wife was no longer around," Barnes went on, "I would have a chance with you. A chance to be happy."

It can't be true, he screamed silently. It can't be.

"And by the time my good half won out," the counselor finished, "it was too late, you see? She was dead already, poor thing, all the life squeezed out of her. Just like all the others the Borg had slaughtered."

Sisko could see his wife lying there under a hideous pile of debris. Eyes staring, mouth open as if she wanted to scream. *Jennifer,* he thought with a jolt of pain. *My beautiful, sweet Jennifer.*

The counselor averted his gaze. "She was beyond anyone's help, Benjamin. And I couldn't stay there. You understand that, don't you? I was ashamed, but I had to run away."

The captain reeled with the significance of Barnes's confession. The woman could have prevented his wife's death, he told himself. She could have given Jennifer a chance to survive.

But she hadn't done it. The counselor had walked away and left Jennifer to die in agony—because she *loved* him. Because some dark, maniacal part of her hated the competition Jennifer represented.

Barnes looked up at him, her eyes full of pain. "Please, Benjamin. It's too late for her, but not for us. We can still be together in the time we have left. It's not too late, I swear it."

Sisko shook his head. It was too much for him to bear. If Barnes had never seen him on the *Saratoga,* had never developed these feelings for him, his wife might be alive today. She might have been *saved.*

"Don't be angry with me," the counselor implored. She touched her fingertips to his chest—lightly, like a lover. "Please, Benjamin. I only wanted us to be together. I only wanted it to be the two of us."

Enraged, Sisko slapped her hand away. He wanted to make her pay for what she had done—for what she *hadn't* done. He wanted her to feel the kind of anguish he was feeling.

Then he looked at her—looked into her eyes. In the darkness of them, he could see a tortured and guilt-twisted soul, who in her own way had borne a burden of pain as heavy as his own.

He couldn't hate Constance Barnes, not any more than Jennifer would have hated her. He wanted to, but he couldn't. Like water in a sieve, his anger gradually drained away.

"There's so little time," the counselor entreated, raising her fingers to his face. "So little time . . ."

For what? he asked himself. A relationship? Even in her madness, even as she framed the words, she had to know that was impossible.

Then abruptly, he realized what she *really* wanted of him. Not romance—not really. It was something else she needed. And he alone had the power to give it to her.

Submerging his bitterness, the captain reached out to her. With unfeeling arms and hands, he embraced her. And slowly, with infinite sadness, he drew her to him.

"It's all right," he told her. "It's all right now."

The counselor looked up at him, hope shining tentatively in her smile. "Oh, Benjamin. I've waited so long to tell you this. So very *long.*"

"I know," Sisko told her, stroking her hair. "And I . . ." He swallowed. "I forgive you."

Resting her head against his chest, she began to sob again. In fact, Barnes trembled with the force of it like a leaf in an autumn storm. Finally, after all these years, the woman had found some measure of relief from her awful burden—some respite from the demons that haunted her.

She had found . . . forgiveness.

And if she was slated to die scant minutes later, that didn't seem to matter to her. All that mattered was she had confessed her sin to the one man who could give her absolution.

Gently the captain guided Barnes to her seat. Then, taking one himself at the conn console, he checked the status of the probes preparatory to launch.

His monitors were supposed to show him that all systems were functioning. But they didn't. They showed him that something was wrong.

The probes were fine, apparently. But the launch

mechanism was off-line. Running a quick diagnostic, he saw why.

"What's the matter?" asked Barnes, still in a daze—but not so much that she couldn't tell there was a problem.

Sisko glanced at her. "We're having a problem. I can't get the launch mechanism to respond."

The counselor's brows met over the bridge of her delicate nose. "But if the probes aren't launched—"

"They won't leave the nexus," he said. "And no one will be saved."

Purposefully he punched a padd on the console, then got up and took Barnes's hand. She looked surprised.

"Where are we going?" she asked.

"You'll see," was all he told her.

Sisko waited for the turbolift to take them to deck four, where the computer diagnostic had pinpointed the trouble with the probe launch. When the lift doors opened, he emerged and took Barnes with him.

"Where are we going?" she asked for the fifth or sixth time—he had lost count. But he had no time to provide explanations.

Instead he pulled her along the corridor behind him. They turned right and then left, following the contours of the hull. Finally the captain caught sight of his objective.

At first it looked only like a shadow among all the other shadows in this minimally lit space. Then he got closer, and he could see the shadow was shaped like a man.

What's more, on the deck beside it, there was a section of bulkhead lying on its side. The elaborate command circuitry underneath it had been exposed, and it was this the man-shaped shadow seemed to be working on.

Clearly someone was sabotaging the launch, and the captain had a pretty good idea who it might be. One of his former colleagues on the old *Saratoga*. One of the few people in the galaxy he would have trusted with everything he held dear.

And he would have been wrong to do so. Because this particular former colleague had sold him out, along with all their other old friends. His mouth twisting with anger, he called out a single name.

"Lopez!"

The corridor rang and echoed with the name, though in this case it was more of an accusation. The science officer turned around. Even in the meager light, there was no mistaking his features.

"In the flesh," Lopez confirmed.

He was holding an engineering tool—one he could have obtained in any one of a dozen places. What's more, the science officer would have been familiar with all of them, since most ships were alike in that regard—and the science and engineering sections often worked hand in hand.

Sisko nodded. "I should have known. You were the one piloting the *Defiant* when we ran into trouble.

You could have taken us right into the nexus, regardless of whatever course Thorn had plotted for you."

Lopez smiled grimly. "Could have and *did,* I'm afraid."

Barnes turned to the captain. She was trying hard to grasp what was happening, even in her madness. "You mean this is all *Lopez's* fault? He was the one who got us stuck here?"

"That's correct," the science officer informed her. "But not before I'd disabled the inertial dampers on the pod deck, so there wouldn't be any easy way out for us."

She shook her head, obviously puzzled and confused. "But why? Why would you do such a thing?"

"A good question," Lopez agreed. "And while we're at it, here are a couple more. Why have I not used one of the probes to escape? Why have I lingered here, to face certain death along with the rest of you?"

"Why indeed," said Sisko, thinking it through, "unless . . . we're not going to die, after all."

The science officer chuckled. "Very good, sir. Your reasoning is impeccable, as always."

Barnes looked more disoriented than ever. "How can that be? We exhausted every way we could think of to help ourselves. The probes were our very last chance."

"To help *ourselves,* yes," Lopez advised her. "But if you were to consult the ship's long-range sensors, you would find that *outside* help is on the way."

The captain looked up at the intercom grid. "Computer, is there a vessel approaching us? And if so, what kind of vessel is it?"

"Sensors indicate the approach of three Retizian trading ships," the computer responded. "All are equipped with Starfleet analog warp engines and level-three tactical systems."

Sisko frowned. With level-three armaments, they might be a match for even a healthy *Defiant*. "I still don't understand," he confessed.

"I'll spell it out for you," Lopez offered magnanimously. "At this point there's no reason to keep any of it a secret, is there?" He shrugged. "As you know, I'm a man of rather extravagant vices."

The captain grunted. "Your obsession with women, you mean."

"That is my primary vice, yes," the science officer replied. "But I have another, which comes in a close second. And that, my friend, is gambling—on anything and everything. I won't bore you with the details, but it got me into trouble recently. Big trouble, actually, because I became indebted to the Retizians—who don't take such things lightly."

"You could have come to me," Sisko noted. "I could have helped."

Lopez shook his head. "My losses were huge. You couldn't have made a dent in them. And of course, neither could I—at least, not with legal tender. However, I did have *one* thing of value to bargain with: your *blood*."

"My blood?" the captain echoed.

"That's right," the science officer responded. "As

you'll recall, every one of our old colleagues aboard this vessel—with the exception of myself and Counselor Barnes here—was on an away team sent down to Thetalian Prime some years ago. You were there. Thorn was there. So were Lieutenant Commander Graal, Dr. Laffer, and Lieutenant Zar."

Sisko recalled the incident. It wasn't a pretty one. And what came after wasn't pretty either.

"We contracted a disease," he said.

"So you did," Lopez agreed. "A particularly vicious disease, as I understand it. You almost died. If not for Dr. Laffer, you most certainly would have. But you survived, all of you—though you still carry the microscopic organisms responsible for the disease in your blood."

Sisko was beginning to figure it out. "Corlandium."

Barnes was still in the dark. She said so.

"Corlandium," the captain explained, "is a mineral found only on Thetalian Prime. It's worth a million times its weight in gold-pressed latinum. And the organisms we still carry in our blood secrete corlandium on a regular basis—even if it's only in trace amounts."

Understanding dawned on the counselor's face. She stared at Lopez, incredulous. "You're paying off your debts with this stuff?"

"Not the stuff itself," said the science officer. "Rather, the organisms that create it. Unfortunately the tiny things are exceptionally fragile. Particular, one might say, about where they live."

"They're partial to humans, Bolians, Klingons, and

several other races," Sisko pointed out. "But not Retizians."

Lopez nodded. "Unfortunately for the Retizians. And the organisms absolutely detest any kind of artificial environment."

Sisko glared at his former colleague. "So we're going to be habitats for the organisms. Places where they can continue to thrive—and more to the point, where they can produce corlandium."

"My god," said Barnes, her features pinched with disgust.

"You'll be more than habitats," Lopez told him. "You'll be breeding grounds. The Retizians think they can make the organisms multiply again, despite the antibodies in your systems. If so, they can step up corlandium production exponentially—and with the judicious use of drugs, still keep you healthy and viable."

"Healthy zombies," Sisko corrected.

"If you prefer," Lopez conceded amiably.

"You're a monster," the counselor rasped.

The science officer turned to her, his expression deadly serious all of a sudden. "No," he insisted. "I'm a desperate man."

Sisko believed it. Lopez had never done anything even remotely like this in his stint on the *Saratoga*.

"Believe me," said the science officer, "I wish things had turned out otherwise. I had no desire to hurt anyone, much less my old friends. But I love life too much to let it go without a fight."

"So do we," said a deep, angry voice.

Lopez's head snapped around. He stared at the source of the voice, his mouth open, his face losing color by the second.

Sisko turned, too—and saw Aidan Thorn striding down the corridor to join them, his mouth twisted with barely bridled fury. He wasn't alone, either. Zar was right on his heels.

"A-Aidan," the science officer stammered. He tried to smile. "You don't understand. All I was trying to do—"

Before Lopez could finish his explanation, Thorn landed a crushing blow to his jaw. The science officer bounced off the bulkhead behind him and sank to the deck, blood trickling from the corner of his mouth.

The captain got between the two of them in a hurry, but it was all he could do to keep Thorn from belting Lopez a second time. After all, the security officer was every bit as strong as he looked.

"Come on," said Zar, using his Bolian strength to aid Sisko in his efforts to restrain Thorn. "That's not going to accomplish anything, Aidan."

"It'll make me *feel* better," Thorn snarled. He pointed an accusing finger at his old comrade, who was only now dragging himself to his knees. "You're scum, Lopez. You're worse than scum. If I'd known what a low-life bastard you were, I never would have saved your life so often."

The science officer wiped his mouth with the back of his hand and placed his other hand against the bulkhead for support. Then, with something of an effort, he got to his feet.

"Yes," he said, glancing at the big man. "I suppose those seem like errors in judgment now, under the circumstances."

"To all of us," Sisko commented. He turned to Zar. "You heard everything, I take it?"

The Bolian nodded. "Everything. Just as you intended when you opened a link to the probes' comm systems. I'm assuming you punched a communications padd up on the bridge?"

"You're assuming right," Sisko confirmed.

Lopez nodded. "Clever, my friend. But in the long run, it doesn't matter. The Retizians are on their way. And as far as they're concerned, the bargain is sealed."

Zar looked to the captain. "Any ideas?"

As if on cue, Sisko was paged over the intercom system. It was O'Brien.

He smiled. "Go ahead, Chief. I'm listening."

"Dax and I have effected repairs," O'Brien reported. "We're ready to take the *Defiant* out of here."

"Do it, Chief," the captain told him. "I'll meet you on the bridge as soon as I can."

A moment later, he could feel the reassuring hum of the impulse engines through the *Defiant*'s deck plates. His old comrades looked at him quizzically. The last either of them had heard, fixing the propulsion system was an impossibility.

"The engines," said Thorn, his eyes widening. "Either I'm crazy or they're back on line."

"You're not crazy," Sisko assured him, a part of him secretly enjoying the look on the big man's face.

"Then we can leave the nexus under our own power," the Bolian concluded, obviously caught between surprise and amusement.

He had barely gotten the words out when they felt the ship move. It was a subtle sensation, even with some of the inertial dampers out of commission, but there was no mistaking it.

"I guess that answers my question," said Zar.

Lopez, meanwhile, was white as a sheet. He'd obviously expected to come out on top, even after Thorn and the Bolian arrived. Now he saw his victory wasn't nearly as certain as he'd believed.

The science officer shook his head. "I don't get it. I thought the engines were damaged beyond repair."

"They were damaged," the captain confirmed, "but not beyond repair. Oh, at first, we were in a genuine bind, no doubt about it. Then our engineering team came up with the idea of replicating those damaged engine parts."

"An idea that failed," said Thorn. He looked at Zar, then at Sisko again. "At least, that's what I thought."

"Actually," Sisko told him, "I asked Chief O'Brien to hold a key component back—and replace it with junk. Hence the appearance that we were still dead in the water."

"But why?" the big man pressed. Then he answered his own question. "Unless you suspected sabotage—and wanted to give the one responsible a chance to reveal himself."

Sisko nodded. "Exactly, Mr. Thorn. Chief O'Brien and Lieutenant Commander Graal found Lopez's handiwork on the pod deck shortly before we hit the wave nexus. At the time, we didn't know quite what to make of it, of course. But when we hit the nexus, we knew."

Zar shook his head. "Then the whole time, you and O'Brien and Graal were deceiving us—making us think we were doomed so you could flush out the traitor among us."

"As it happens," said the captain, "Lieutenant Dax was in on it, too. But we can discuss all this later." He jerked a thumb in the direction of the nearest turbo-lift. "Right now, we've got some Retizians to deal with, and I don't think they'll take no for an answer."

CHAPTER
17

As Sisko emerged onto the bridge, leading his former colleagues, he saw the viewscreen was still a confusion of bright colors. Also, that O'Brien and Dax were at Ops and Conn, respectively.

He acknowledged them with a nod. They nodded back.

"Mr. Thorn," he announced, looking back over his shoulder, "keep an eye on our friend Lopez, will you? Make sure he doesn't try anything."

The bearded man, who had armed himself with a phaser on the way up to the bridge, nodded enthusiastically. "With pleasure, Captain."

"Thank you," said Sisko. "Mr. Zar, you've got Tactical."

"Aye, sir," said the Bolian, crossing the bridge with the alacrity of a starving man at a Benzite buffet.

The captain smiled. Zar had maintained his vigil over Laffer without once complaining. But now that Graal was free to keep an eye on the doctor, the Bolian seemed eager to make a *real* contribution.

Besides, next to Sisko himself, Zar was the best tactical officer they had—even better than O'Brien, who had served in that capacity on the *Rutledge*. And in a pinch like this one, they needed all the expertise they could bring to bear.

Barnes took up a position near the lift doors, out of everyone's way. No doubt, thought the captain, she wanted to be of help, too. But in her muddled state, he didn't trust her to handle any of the control panels.

As Sisko sat down in the center seat, he looked to Dax. "What's our speed and heading, Lieutenant?"

"Our heading is two-four-two mark eight," Dax replied. "And we're proceeding at full impulse—which is, of course, all we've got."

The captain leaned back in his chair. There would be no outrunning the Retizians—not on impulse power alone. And the ship's Romulan-designed cloak, which would have come in handy at a time like this, was still completely useless. Pity, he thought.

Sisko wished now that he had devoted some of his resources to the cloaking system's repair. But until the Retizians had entered the picture, he hadn't expected there would be any real need for it.

The captain frowned. Neither speed nor illusion would get them out of this fix. Apparently they would have to win a decisive victory before they could even think about escape. That meant they would have to make up for their obvious disadvantages—and quickly.

Zar turned to him, all business now. "Sir, the energies in the nexus will affect phaser and photon torpedo accuracy. I suggest we refrain from firing until we've emerged from it."

Sisko nodded. "Agreed, Lieutenant." He glanced at Ops. "Where are the Retizians now, Mr. O'Brien?"

"Just outside the phenomenon," the engineer reported. "And I'm reading a great deal of sensor activity, so they must know we're coming."

"I wonder what they make of us," Thorn said. "One minute we're helpless, ripe for the plucking. And the next, we're moving again under our own power—even if it is only impulse."

A good question, thought the captain. If the *Defiant* could muster impulse speeds, the enemy had to be wondering what else they could do. Maybe they could use that element of uncertainty to their advantage.

"What's their range?" he asked O'Brien.

The engineer consulted his instruments. "Eighty-six million kilometers and closing, sir."

Sisko nodded. "Red alert. Shields up."

An instant later, the bridge was bathed in a lurid red light. If any of them hadn't appreciated the seriousness of their plight, the captain was certain they would appreciate it now.

Sitting back in his chair, Sisko rubbed his temple with a forefinger. He was starting to generate some ideas, but he didn't know if they would work—and even if they did, whether any of them would be enough to take out all three of their adversaries.

"Mr. O'Brien," he said out loud. "Can you bypass the damage Mr. Lopez did to the command circuitry?"

The chief turned to him and nodded. "Aye, sir. It shouldn't take more than a minute or so."

"Do it," the captain told him.

Sisko saw Dax dart a glance at him. She was smiling as she uttered a single word: "Decoys."

The captain didn't respond. Instead, he turned to the Bolian. "Mr. Zar, open communication with the probes as soon as they're launched. Speak to them as if there were someone actually aboard each one of them."

Zar grunted appreciatively. Apparently he'd figured it out as well. "Acknowledged, sir. Opening comm link."

"Clever," remarked Lopez. "Very clever indeed."

"No one asked you," said Thorn.

The traitor ignored him. "Being warp capable," he went on, "the probes will be past the Retizians before they know what's happened. They won't have time to analyze the situation—only to react."

"Of course," the Trill added, "they might be surprised by the appearance of passengers on the probes, but they don't dare let them get away—or they take a chance on losing their living corlandium mines."

"The damaged command circuits have been bypassed," O'Brien reported. "Ready to launch any time, sir."

"Program them for a variety of headings," Sisko ordered. "We don't want to make it too easy on the Retizians."

"Various headings," the engineer confirmed.

Sisko tapped his fingers on his armrest, waiting for the right time. Reds and blues stabbed at one another on the viewscreen until they drowned in a yellow-orange tide. Then that gave way as well, to a webwork of dark greens and purples.

"Launch probes," he said at last.

On the screen, the captain could see the probes dart forward at the speed of light, four times as fast as the *Defiant* herself. They were gone before he knew it.

A few seconds later, the image on the screen changed. The roiling colors thinned and faded, giving way to a field of slowly moving stars. Finally, with a last, mighty surge, the *Defiant* tore itself free from the nexus.

What's more, they were in luck. As Sisko had hoped, the Retizians were in visual range—still in the process of wheeling about to pursue the unexpected probes, their warp engines as yet unengaged.

Perfect, the captain thought, just perfect. They couldn't have asked for a better target.

"Mr. Zar, lock on to the vessel to starboard. Fire at will—phasers and photon torpedoes."

The Bolian did as he was instructed. Just before the Retizian could take off at light-speed, the *Defiant*'s barrage hit it in its port quarter, spattering light through the void.

The impact must have jarred something in the

Retizian, because it didn't go to warp alongside its sister ships. And when it began to come about again, presumably in an attempt to face its tormentor, it did so more slowly than it should have.

But before it could complete its maneuver, Zar raked it a second time with the *Defiant*'s firepower. And then a third. As always, the Bolian's marksmanship was a work of art.

"Their shields are down," he announced. "Considerable damage to their weapons and propulsion systems."

Sisko nodded. That was one Retizian they wouldn't have to worry about for a while. But there were still two more, and his ruse wouldn't keep them occupied for very long. Once they realized the probes were empty and unmanned, they would be back—with a vengeance.

"Lieutenant Dax," he said, "withdraw to a point one thousand kilometers inside the nexus. Chief, ready tractor beams."

O'Brien looked back at him, a question in his eyes. But he didn't voice it. He merely followed the captain's orders.

His friend the Trill had to be wondering, too. But like her colleague, she kept her inquiries to herself.

They had barely ducked back inside the nexus when the other two Retizians returned. They wouldn't be very happy about the condition of their sister ship, Sisko mused. He hoped it wouldn't make them too cautious.

A moment later, his wish was granted. Latching on

to the *Defiant* with her targeting systems, one of the Retizians peeled off for a strafing run.

Of course, the Federation ship's position in the nexus would make accuracy a problem, as Zar had indicated earlier—but at close quarters, it wouldn't be a *big* problem. In fact, it would be rather easy.

"Brace yourselves," the captain warned. "You especially, Mr. Thorn. This is going to be as rough as it gets."

His colleagues secured themselves as best they could. Heeding Sisko's advice, Thorn kept an extra-wary eye on Lopez.

The captain took the time to warn Graal as well. After all, she had to brace both herself and Dr. Laffer. And knowing the Craynid, she would need a few more seconds than the rest of them.

Precautions taken, Sisko applied himself to the task at hand. "Mr. O'Brien, target the Retizian. On my mark, activate those tractor beams."

The engineer fiddled with his controls. A couple of seconds later, he looked up. "We're locked on target, sir."

"Ready phasers and torpedoes," Sisko told Zar.

"Ready, sir," came the reply.

The captain's eyes fixed on the viewscreen, where the Retizian was gathering speed for an oblique approach. What he had in mind would require split-second timing and absolute discipline—but he believed his ship and his personnel were up to the task.

On the screen, the Retizian was beginning its run—but at what seemed like a greater speed than Sisko had anticipated. A *much* greater speed.

Checking his monitor, he confirmed the observation. It would make it that much tougher to do what they had to do. Suddenly he had a sick feeling in the pit of his stomach.

Unfortunately it was too late to back off now. Everything was in motion. All they could do was persevere—and hope.

Jaw clenched, the captain waited until the Retizian was right on top of them. Then he barked his commands, the bridge resounding with them.

"Activate tractor beams! Zar—fire!"

What happened next came too fast for the human eye to follow or the human mind to comprehend. The bridge tilted almost on its side, deck plates shivering and bulkheads shrieking, as if giant hands were trying to tear it apart.

Sisko himself went spinning out of his seat, though he managed to grab the base of his control board before he could go very far. Sparks erupted on the opposite side of the bridge, signaling the demise of an empty console. There were curses and cries of pain.

But when it was all over, he shot a look at the viewscreen and realized his plan had worked. The Retizian was withdrawing at half-impulse, its weapons ports charred and fused, only one of its nacelles generating any kind of plasma trail.

The captain tapped his communicator badge. "Sisko to Graal. Are you all right, Commander?"

The Craynid's reply was unusually prompt. "Dr. Laffer and I have sustained no injuries as a result of the impact. In fact, she is beginning to show signs of emerging from her coma."

An unexpected benefit, the captain mused. Still, it was good news—and he would take as much of that as he could get.

Grimly he congratulated himself. He had taken a calculated risk and it had paid off. As he dragged himself to his feet, he replayed the sequence of events in his mind.

First, the *Defiant*'s tractor beams had latched on to the hurtling Retizian, creating—if only for an instant—an inelastic bond between the two. If the Retizian vessel had been a top-of-the-line Federation starship, it might have had enough power to drag the *Defiant* indefinitely.

But as formidable as its tactical systems might have been, the Retizian's propulsion system had been nothing to boast about. Snared by the *Defiant*, it simply dropped out of warp.

And before the Retizian could recover from that development, Zar had implemented the second part of the plan, unleashing the fury of the Federation ship's weapons. And what a fury it was.

The result? One crippled Retizian vessel.

Of course, the *Defiant* had taken its lumps as well. Laboring under the strain of a burden they hadn't been designed for, the tractor generators had been wrecked beyond repair. The structural integrity system had been badly stressed and half the sensors were off-line again.

On top of that, the bridge crew had been roughed up. O'Brien had suffered a cut to his cheek, and Thorn looked to have broken his wrist, causing him to switch his phaser to his other hand.

Nonetheless they had been lucky. The situation could have been worse—much worse—and the captain knew it.

But they weren't out of danger yet. There was still one more Retizian out there—and after what its commander had seen, he wasn't going to give them any room to maneuver. Sisko had scarcely slipped back into the center seat when the last of his adversaries went into action.

As it happened, the captain had planned for this as well. But of all the unorthodox tactics he'd put to use in the last couple of minutes, this one would be the toughest to implement.

Turning to Zar, he said two words: "Guldammur Four."

The Bolian almost smiled—but there wasn't enough time. His fingers flying over his tactical board like a flock of demented birds, he accomplished what he had to do. Finally he looked up.

"Ready, sir," said Zar.

By then, the Retizian was descending on them the way a hawk might descend on a field mouse. Of course, they could have used their impulse capability to make themselves a more difficult target—but Zar's job was tough enough as it was. Going to impulse would have made it impossible.

So they sat. And waited. And despite the calm he was trying to effect, despite his appearance of confidence, Sisko could feel a bead of sweat making its way down the side of his face.

Meanwhile the Retizian was looming larger and larger on the viewscreen. Sisko could see the details of its design, almost down to the texture of its duranium alloy hull. He could read the Retizian designation on its flank, appreciate the artistry in the insignia just below it.

That was when Zar chose to fire. The *Defiant* emitted four simultaneous phaser beams, each one aimed at a different point on the enemy vessel. But they were narrow-gauge beams, incapable of doing much damage even if they made it through the Retizian's defenses.

Suddenly O'Brien cursed. "The shields. They're—"

"It's all right," the captain assured him, holding up a hand for emphasis. "At ease, Chief."

He had noticed the lapse in the *Defiant*'s deflector shields himself, but it hadn't worried him a bit. In fact, it was all part of the plan. And anyway, the shields were up again a second later, the Federation ship none the worse for it.

The Retizian didn't launch a return volley—at least, not right away. It just kept coming closer and closer, until it was on the verge of filling the viewscreen with its bulk.

The ships were forty thousand kilometers apart.

Thirty thousand. Twenty. Ten. Surely, the captain thought, if the Retizian was going to open fire, she would do so now.

But she didn't. Instead, at the last possible second, she veered off. And instead of coming back for a second pass, she took up a position by one of her crippled sister ships.

"I don't understand," said O'Brien, peering at his monitors. And then, abruptly, he figured it out. Eyes narrowing, he turned to Zar. "You dropped our shields so you could effect a transport."

The Bolian nodded. "It was something Captain Sisko and I pulled off once before, on the *Saratoga.* We were in a bind that time, too."

"I remember," Thorn joined in. "We were up against the Breen. Zar fired a narrow-gauge phaser spread to poke a few holes in the enemy's defenses. Then he dropped our shields for an instant and used our transporter to sabotage their weapons banks."

"By beaming over a bunch of junk to clog up their ports," Dax observed. "And thanks to all the engine parts we had to scrap, we had junk to spare." She quirked a smile. "Nice work, Mr. Zar."

O'Brien grunted. *"Very* nice."

The Bolian inclined his head. "I aim to please."

Sisko glanced at the Trill. "Set a course for *Deep Space Nine,* Old Man. It looks like Mars is going to have to wait awhile."

"Aye, Captain," said Dax, implementing his order. From his place by a bulkhead, Lopez shook his head. "Damn," he whispered, clearly bitter about the way things had turned out.

Sisko didn't look at him—not right away. First he made sure the Retizians didn't make a move to stop them as they cruised past at full impulse. Apparently they were every bit as whipped as they looked.

Lopez laughed a disappointed laugh. "You know," he said, "I didn't think even you could get out of this one, Captain. But again, it seems I managed to underestimate you. Seems I'm not much of a gambler." He glanced at O'Brien. "But then, I suppose I should have known that already."

Sisko turned a disapproving glare on him. "You'll have plenty of time to express your admiration before a court-martial, Lieutenant." He tilted his head to indicate the turbolift. "Mr. Thorn—throw our former colleague in the brig. I believe his shift on the bridge is over."

The big man smiled despite the pain of his broken wrist. "Aye, sir. Now that you mention it, I believe it is."

Yet as Thorn escorted Lopez into the lift, the captain derived no pleasure from it. Once, the science officer had been his friend, and it never felt good to lose one of those—no matter the circumstances.

Out of the corner of his eye, Sisko saw Barnes approaching him. He would have almost preferred to face another batch of Retizians than see the look on her face. But he turned to her nonetheless.

"Benjamin?" she said, her eyes pleading with him.

Though she had remained quiet, she must have been very frightened. "Is it over now?"

He nodded. "Yes, Counselor. It's over. We're going home."

Barnes regarded him for a moment. She looked as if she was on the verge of asking another question, but she never asked it. Apparently, even in her muddled state, she had figured out what the answer would be.

Looking terribly sad, the counselor turned and made her way toward the turbolift. The captain felt badly for her, but he knew it would send the wrong signal if he got up and went after her—and the woman had been through enough misery for one lifetime.

He was about to ask Dax to assist Barnes when the Trill held her hand up, signaling that it wouldn't be necessary. Slaving her console to O'Brien's, she hurried after the counselor and caught up with her just as the lift doors were opening.

Barnes looked at Dax for a moment, but without the rancor the counselor had exhibited earlier. In fact, there wasn't even a flicker of recognition. The Trill put her arm around the other woman's shoulder.

"Come on," she said. "You seem to have a lot on your mind, and I can be a pretty good listener."

Barnes nodded, her eyes wide and chillingly child-like. "Thank you," she replied gratefully.

Then they too vanished into the lift. Sisko sighed. The counselor was going to need some therapy before she could even think about returning to duty. Captain Kyprios was going to be terribly disappointed.

Abruptly he realized Zar was looking at him. O'Brien as well. Neither of them understood what had happened to Barnes. But then, neither of them had been on the bridge earlier when she made her bizarre admissions.

"I'll fill you in later," he told them. "I promise."

Right now he just wanted to sit here. To gather his thoughts, as they limped back to the station as best they could. And to try to heal the wounds the counselor had reopened.

He swallowed. *Jennifer* . . .

CHAPTER 18

JAKE SISKO STOOD by an airlock in the upper docking pylon and peered through the transparent portion of the inner door. Beside him, his friend Nog did the same thing.

Somewhere out in space, the *Defiant* was headed their way—battered and beaten up, but still in one piece. Anyway, that's what he had heard.

"Can you see them yet?" asked the boy.

"No," said the Ferengi, squinting as if that would help. "Can you?"

Jake shook his head. "They were supposed to be here by now. At least, that's what Major Kira told me."

"And she wasn't lying," said a feminine voice from behind them.

Turning, they saw it was Kira herself, no doubt here

to welcome her commanding officer back to the station. And she had Dr. Bashir with her.

"Apparently," the doctor explained, "there was a little trouble with the warp drive Mr. O'Brien cobbled together en route. And since the *Defiant* was already so close to home, Captain Sisko decided to shut it down and not take any chances."

"Just what I would have done," Nog commented sagely.

Bashir smiled. "In any case, they shouldn't be delayed more than a few minutes. They were only traveling at warp factor one to begin with. Apparently, after what the *Defiant* had been through, that was all the strain her structural integrity field could take."

Jake wasn't exactly comforted by the comment. Structural integrity fields were serious business. Without them, a ship's hull would be left to its own devices—and those weren't nearly sufficient to stand the incredible stresses of warp-speed travel.

Deep down, the doctor had to be worried as well. But for the boy's sake, he was doing his best not to show it.

Abruptly something out in the void caught Jake's eye. Leaning closer to the transparent barrier, he focused on it. Concentrated on it. And before long he found himself grinning.

"It's the *Defiant,*" he announced, unable to keep the mounting excitement out of his voice.

"So it is," Kira confirmed.

The starship was moving at only a fraction of

impulse speed as it approached *Deep Space Nine*. But then, that would be the case no matter what shape its warp drive was in. As the boy looked on, the *Defiant* switched to its thruster array.

After what seemed like much too long a time, the *Defiant* nudged up against the docking pylon. A tractor lock was established and clamps were applied. And an eternity later, the outside door on the airlock rolled aside.

The first ones out of the airlock were Dax, O'Brien, and Dr. Laffer. The Trill and the engineer were positioned on either side of the doctor, who still looked pale and a little shaky after her ordeal.

Bashir came forward to take Laffer's arm. "Come," he said. "I'll escort you to the infirmary."

His colleague made a sound of contempt. "And who said I needed to visit the infirmary?" she asked.

Bashir's eyes narrowed purposefully. *"I* did, Doctor. After all, you suffered a severe head trauma, you were unconscious for several hours, and your biosigns dropped so low they at one point could barely be detected. The only reason you're up and about is you've pumped yourself full of tropazine or something equally insidious."

Laffer opened her mouth to speak, but Bashir held a finger up. When he continued, his voice was even more stern and unyielding.

"You have two choices, Doctor. You can come to the infirmary under your own power or I can toss you over my shoulder and carry you there—and don't make the mistake of thinking I won't do it."

Laffer regarded him with a mixture of surprise and curiosity. For the very first time since Jake had met her, the doctor didn't have a caustic response at her fingertips.

"If that's how you feel about it," she said.

"It is," Bashir confirmed.

Taking Laffer's arm, he led her down the corridor toward the turbolift. What's more, she didn't utter a sound the whole time.

O'Brien scratched his head as he watched them go. "How about that?" he said. "I guess no one had ever gotten firm with her before."

"I guess," Dax echoed. "Although she's probably a little more docile when she's recovering from a coma."

Jake saw Graal come up quietly behind O'Brien and tap him on the shoulder. Instantly the human whirled. Then he saw who it was. Taking a deep breath, he contained his temper.

"For the love o' Mike," grated O'Brien, "I asked you not to sneak up on me like that, Commander."

The Craynid eyed him for a moment with those round black eyes of hers. Then she replied in her slow, whistling way, "I only wished to compliment you on a job well done."

Now, apparently, it was O'Brien's turn to be surprised. "Well," he said, "thank you. I appreciate that. Especially when it comes from someone whose opinion I've grown to respect."

Graal nodded. "See you later," she told him. Then

she moved past him and followed the doctors down the corridor.

Kira looked at Dax. "It must have been an interesting trip."

The Trill grunted in response. "If that's interesting, I wouldn't mind taking a boring one once in a while." She turned to her friend. "Incidentally, have you heard anything from Odo?"

"Not yet," the Bajoran answered.

"Odo will do just fine," Nog assured the women. "After all, he's got my father with him."

That's what they're afraid of, Jake thought.

However, he was only listening to their conversation with one ear. The rest of him was still intent on the *Defiant*'s open hatchway, where someone else was making his exit.

As it turned out, it was two someones. Chief Thorn—and Lieutenant Lopez. The big man was holding a phaser on the science officer as they made their way through the airlock.

Catching sight of the boy, Lopez stopped for a moment, as if he wanted to say something. But he couldn't seem to find the words—couldn't seem to come up with anything even approaching an explanation.

He just shrugged, as if by way of an apology, and resumed his journey. And Thorn stayed right behind him, taking no chances.

Jake sighed. He'd liked Lopez a lot. It was hard for him to understand how one of the good guys could suddenly become one of the bad guys. It was probably one of those lessons his father was always talking about—the kind a person could learn only from experience.

Then someone else came out of the airlock. Counselor Barnes, the boy thought. But she looked different somehow. Hollow-eyed, distracted, as if she'd taken more of a beating on the *Defiant* than the others.

Gently, Dax took the counselor's arm and led her away. Barnes looked around, but she didn't say a word. Not one.

Kira looked at O'Brien. "You think she'll be all right?"

The engineer shrugged sadly. "In time, I suppose."

Then the two of them glanced at Jake and Nog, and clammed up like Ornathian winterblossoms in a cold spell. Apparently this was one of those things teenagers weren't supposed to hear about.

Still, the boy had seen the counselor's eyes. He had an idea it was something bad.

It made him even more concerned about his father. Kira had said the captain was all right, but "all right" covered a wide range of possibilities. Biting his lip, Jake peered deeper into the airlock.

A moment later, his vigilance was rewarded. Sisko himself appeared, with Lieutenant Zar right behind him. When he saw his son waiting for him, the captain's eyes lit up.

Jake felt a lump in his throat. The whole time his father and the others had been in danger, he'd been hanging around the station with Nog. He hadn't known about the wave nexus—no one had.

Then Zar called to tell Kira they weren't going to Mars after all, and a few minutes later Kira passed the information to Jake. At the time, he'd felt funny about it. Off balance, somehow.

Sure the problem was over, and he was relieved. But deep down, where the irrational rules, the boy was still worried—still chilled to the bone with fear. And he knew he would have to see his father before he could get past that fear.

He was past it now. His father was hale and whole, just as he had hoped. The captain came forward and wrapped his arms around his son and hugged him. Jake hugged just as hard.

"Welcome home, Dad."

Over his father's shoulder, he could see Zar looking on approvingly. The Bolian winked and the boy winked back.

"Thanks," said the captain. "It's good to *be* home."

Abruptly a voice filled the corridor. "Ops to Major Kira."

The Bajoran tapped her communicator badge. "Kira here. What can I do for you, Mr. Leskanic?"

"Major, we're in contact with Security Chief Odo."

Kira looked to Sisko, then O'Brien. She looked positively grim.

"Patch me through," she said.

There was a pause. Then the familiar voice of the shapeshifter replaced Lieutenant Leskanic's. "Odo here."

The major frowned. "How did it go, Odo?"

Of course, Jake knew exactly what she was asking about. Half the personnel on the station knew—and they had all been rooting for the constable to get those power coils.

Again there was a pause. Then Odo gave Kira her answer.

"It appears Karvis will be dry this spring, Major—and for many springs to come. The power coils are on their way."

Kira broke out into a smile. "That's wonderful news," she told the constable. "Just wonderful. I don't know how to thank you, Odo."

The shapeshifter grunted. "You can thank me," he replied, "by never—and I mean never—asking me to do anything like this again."

Jake laughed. So did his father and Major Kira and Chief O'Brien. In fact, their laughter filled the corridor from one end to the other.

Nog harrumphed. "I don't see what's so funny," he insisted.

But he was the only one.

Dax sat down across from Thorn and deposited their drinks on the table between them. His was a synthale, hers a Modvaarian tonic.

"Cheers," she said, raising her glass.

"Cheers," he agreed, and downed the synthale at a single swallow. A little of it trickled into his beard and he wiped it away with his hand.

The Trill was far from demure when it came to imbibing, but this time she just sipped at her drink. "So," she said, "I understand the commissioning of the *Saratoga* will be delayed a few days."

Thorn nodded. "Until Dr. Laffer fully recovers. Now that Counselor Barnes won't be joining us and my good friend Lopez is headed for a penal colony, we need every old colleague we can lay our hands on."

The mention of Lopez clearly made the security chief uncomfortable. But then, he and the science officer had been close for years. It must have been jarring for him to find out how wrong he'd been about the man.

Dax smiled. "I see your point."

Thorn considered his empty glass. "You know, I've been a security officer for a long time. After a while, you develop a sense about people—an intuition, if you like."

She saw what he was getting at. "And while you'd love to think I invited you for a drink to hear your war tales, you've got a feeling that's not the case. Is that it?"

He looked at her with his tiny blue eyes. "In a nutshell, yes."

The Trill shrugged. "I have to admit, I was wondering about something—something you told me on the *Defiant.*" She could feel herself blushing a little. "In fact, Mr. Thorn—"

"Aidan," he insisted.

Dax began again. "In fact, Aidan, to tell you the truth, it made me suspect *you* were the saboteur."

Thorn's eyes opened wide with surprise. "Me?" he replied. "A traitor to my friends? You've got to be joking."

She shook her head from side to side. "Not at all. After all, you charted the course that brought us smack up against the wave nexus. Or at least, that's what I thought."

The bearded man grunted. "Except it was Lopez who advised me how to navigate that leg of the journey. He said he knew that part of space a bit better than I did. And I've had told you that, too, if I'd had an inkling someone was suspected of sabotage."

"Which you didn't," Dax agreed. "Unfortunately we had to keep our suspicions a secret."

He stroked his chin. "Is that why I was teamed up with O'Brien and Graal? So they could keep an eye on me?"

The Trill nodded. "I'm afraid so—though now that we know what we know, I feel kind of foolish about it. Still," she said, leaning forward, "I'd like to know why you lied to me."

The big man looked at her askance. "Lied? About what?"

"About our mutual friend," Dax explained. "Simora—the Vulcan you'd met on the *Victory?* You said she didn't take kindly to humans—when she seemed to me to be very happy to be among humans."

Thorn's expression became one of embarrassment.

259

"Ah," he replied. *"That.* I guess it's my turn to apologize now."

The Trill's eyes narrowed. "Then you *did* lie to me?"

He sighed. "Yes. And don't think I don't regret it. But I think you'll agree I had a good reason."

And he went on to tell her what it was.

It was good to be back, Odo thought, sitting down at his desk and leaning back in his chair—and it wasn't just because he felt a duty to the station. Ultimately the shapeshifter was a being for whom travel held no particular appeal and faraway places no special allure.

In short, he was a homebody, and he had no regrets about it. Let others encounter unknown races and civilizations, he thought. He liked it right here on *Deep Space Nine.*

Abruptly the doors to his office slid aside and Quark walked in, completely recovered from his malady. At any rate, that was the effect of the report Dr. Bashir had issued in Odo's absence.

"Quark," said the constable, eyeing the bartender. "I'm glad to see you're looking fit again."

"So am I," the Ferengi told him. "Though, as I understand it, my health was no impediment to a little transaction with Fel Jangor."

Odo grunted. "If you're referring to my masquerade, that's true. Rom and I obtained the power coils for Major Kira's friend. I guess you could say we accomplished our mission."

"Mind you," said Quark, "I was concerned about that. In fact, it was the first thing that crossed my mind when I woke up in sickbay."

"I'm sure it was," the constable told him. "And I'm certain Major Kira appreciated your level of concern."

"I hope so," the Ferengi responded. "After all, we are a family here. And as in any family, a little gratitude goes a long way."

"You'll have to work that out with her," Odo advised.

"Of course," said the Ferengi. No doubt he was already making a mental note of it.

"Will there be anything else?" the constable asked. "Some of us have work to do, you know."

"Actually, there is something," Quark confessed. He assumed a strangely conspiratorial expression. "Tell me, what was it like?"

Odo looked at him. "What was *what* like?"

The Ferengi leaned forward, across the constable's desk. "You know. To be the galaxy's most clever businessman."

Odo's first impulse was to throw the bartender out of his office. Then he remembered what he had done, and he smiled.

"Actually, I rather liked it," he said.

Quark looked surprised. "You did? I mean, of course you did. Who wouldn't?" He tilted his head. "What, exactly, did you like about it?"

Odo considered the question. "I don't know. The

power, perhaps. The sense of opportunity. The feeling that I could get anything I want, if I was inclined to be devious and underhanded enough."

The Ferengi's eyes narrowed in disbelief. "That appealed to you? To *you?*" There was a note of skepticism in his voice—to put it mildly.

The constable nodded. "Believe me, I was as surprised as you are. But I was so taken with my newfound freedom that I exercised it again. That is, just before I returned to the station."

Quark's brow furrowed. "Oh?"

"Oh yes," Odo told him. "While your brother was gorging himself on the buffet, I received a communication from another old friend of yours. I wasn't sure how he tracked me down—or rather, tracked *you* down—but it seems he had his ways."

Quark regarded him. "An old friend, you say?"

"That's correct. A Tyrhennian named Norslat, as it happens—though I recall thinking he was rather slender for a Tyrhennian. In any case, he was inquiring about a supply of machine parts he thought you might have in stock."

"Machine parts?" the Ferengi echoed. He produced a handkerchief and used it to dab at his forehead. *"Which* machine parts?"

The shapeshifter pretended to think. "Ah," he said after a moment. "I remember now. They were vectored resistance nodules. The duranium-coated kind, rated for deep-space applications."

Quark seemed relieved. "You sold Norslat my resistance nodules? I've been trying to get rid of those things forever."

"Well," Odo explained, "you did seem to have them in great abundance. I didn't think it would hurt you to part with a few."

"I see," said the Ferengi, brightening even more. "And Norslat didn't question your appearance? The vagueness of your—I mean *my* features?"

"Certainly he questioned it," the constable replied. "But I blamed it on the quality of the transmission. He seemed to accept that. And before long, we'd cut a deal."

"For how many?" Quark inquired, unable to conceal his eagerness.

"All of them," Odo said. "I tried to hold some back, but he wouldn't settle for less than the entire supply."

Quark rubbed his hands together. "I see. And how much did you get for the little thingamajigs?"

The constable leaned back in his chair and affected a look of pride. "Ten bars of latinum," he announced.

The Ferengi's jaw dropped in joyous incredulity. For a moment, he seemed speechless. "Apiece?" he exclaimed at last. "Why . . . that's incredible!"

Odo shook his head. "Not apiece, Quark. All *together.*"

Suddenly the bartender's expression changed. The fire left his eyes and the color went out of his cheeks.

"All together?" he giggled nervously. "You're kidding, right?"

"I've never been more serious in my life," the constable assured him.

Quark shook his head. "But . . . I paid a *hundred* bars of latinum for those resistance nodules. You only got ten percent of my investment back."

Odo pretended to think again. "That's not good, is it?"

Seeking a means of escape, Quark's eyes darted about like those of a cornered animal. "I know," he blurted. "I'll tell Norslat the truth—that it wasn't me who cut the deal. I'll tell him it was some meddlesome shapeshifter, who had no idea what he was doing."

"I wouldn't advise that," said the constable. "Your friend Jangor might get wind of it and start to wonder with whom he was negotiating—you or a meddlesome shapeshifter. And if he reneged as a result, Major Kira's friends wouldn't get their power coils."

"The *hell* with their power coils," Quark squealed. "I'm out ninety bars of latinum!"

He started out of Odo's office, no doubt to fall on Norslat's mercy as quickly as possible. However, the shapeshifter turned himself into a liquid stream and rematerialized at the door—blocking the Ferengi's way.

"Let me go," cried Quark, his fingers balled into little fists. "I've got to squelch that deal!"

"Not so fast," Odo said sternly. "You may not care what happens to the major's friends—but *I* do."

The Ferengi started to say something else—then stopped. No doubt he'd noticed the changeling's lack of flexibility on this point.

Quark made a sound of frustration deep in his throat. "You're a cruel man, Constable."

"It's part of my job," Odo reminded him.

Muttering something colorful beneath his breath, the Ferengi turned and walked out. The changeling watched him go with some satisfaction. After all, he had been aware for some time that Quark had acquired those nodules illegally. Unfortunately, he had been unable to prove it.

Now, he wouldn't have to. Justice had already been served.

Sisko looked at Zar. "Disappointed?" he echoed.

The Bolian nodded. "Uh-huh."

They were walking along the upper level of the Promenade, looking down on the milling throng that had just arrived via a Pandrilite-Tarquinian trading vessel. The Pandrilites were blue-skinned, not unlike Zar—but much larger. The Tarquinians were small, pale, and mousy-looking.

"You mean in Lopez?" the captain asked.

Zar shook his head. "No, that's not what I'm talking about."

"Then what?" asked Sisko. "I mean, we all got out of our predicament with our skins, didn't we?"

"You don't understand," said his companion. "I'm disappointed in *you.*"

The captain smiled defensively. "Me? For god sakes, why?"

The Bolian returned his gaze. "Because you didn't trust me as you trusted Dax and O'Brien. After all that time on the *Saratoga,* after all we'd been through together, I should probably be offended."

Sisko put a reassuring hand on Zar's shoulder. "Don't be," he recommended. "I would have loved to confide in you."

The Bolian harrumphed. "But you couldn't."

"That's right," said the captain. "Just as I couldn't confide in Graal or Thorn or Lopez. Hard as it was to imagine, *one* of you was playing fast and loose with the lives of the others. I couldn't let my friendships keep me from finding out which one."

Zar frowned at him. "You're going to tell me you really *believed* I could be the culprit? Even for a second?"

Sisko shrugged. "For several seconds. The only one I had a *really* hard time distrusting was Graal. There hasn't been a recorded incident of Craynid duplicity in several hundred years, you know."

"But you didn't tell her, either," the Bolian observed.

"That's right," Sisko confirmed. "Because she might have given something away unintentionally. Bad enough there were already three of us who could have done that. A fourth . . ." He let his voice trail off, his point made.

Zar sighed. "I see what you mean—I think."

Down below, the captain caught a glimpse of their friend Thorn. The man was dickering with a tall, lean Rythrian over some trinket.

"One thing still needs to be resolved," Sisko noted.

"What's that?" asked the Bolian.

The captain pointed to Thorn. "Aidan lied to Dax." He went on to describe the nature of the lie, and the circumstances surrounding it. "I still don't get it."

Zar grunted. "If he didn't know the Vulcan, why pretend that he did?"

"Precisely," Sisko replied.

"Well," said the Bolian, "that's one mystery I can clear up for you. You see, Thorn confided in me recently." He cast his friend a sidelong glance. "At least *someone* does that from time to time."

The captain shook his head ruefully. "You're never going to let me forget this, are you?"

"That's true," Zar told him. "I'm not."

"All right, then," said Sisko. "I'm just going to have to live with it. Now, about Thorn . . . ?"

"It's simple," the Bolian explained. "He's suffering from memory losses. Some big, some little. Some recent, some from a long time ago. And the worst part is, they're irreversible."

The captain felt a wave of compassion for his former security officer. "How did this happen?" he wondered.

"A few years back," Zar responded, "the *Gorkon* encountered an unidentified derelict. It seemed to have been disabled a long time ago, though it wasn't clear why. And since the atmosphere was intact, the crew had rotted away to almost nothing. Starfleet still doesn't know whose ship it was.

"In any case, Thorn was part of the away team that investigated. While he was tinkering with one of the vessel's control consoles, he received some kind of shock. It knocked him out. By the time he reached sickbay, he had pretty much recovered. The chief medical officer couldn't find anything wrong with him. . . ."

"But he'd begun to forget things," Sisko offered.

The Bolian nodded. "Of course, Thorn was the only one who knew it. It didn't show up in any of his routine physicals, and he himself chose not to speak about it."

The captain understood. "Because it would have forced him to give up his commission on the *Gorkon*. And he didn't want that to happen. He wanted to remain in space."

"For a while, anyway." Zar smiled wistfully. "Oh, he knows he'll eventually have to retire and do something else with his life—but in the meantime, he'll enjoy a few good months with the fleet he's always served so proudly." He paused. "That is, if we keep his secret."

Sisko thought about it. There was no way he could see Thorn's condition endangering anyone. Whatever the security officer forgot, he could look up with the help of the ship's computer.

It was only the nuances of life, the flavors and textures and poignancies of each event that would be lost to him. But then, that's where his comrades came in.

To remind him of these things. To tell him what they had been like.

Zar looked at the captain. "We *are* going to keep his secret, aren't we?"

Sisko nodded. "I think so. After all," he asked soberly, watching Thorn continue along the Promenade, "isn't that what friends are for?"

Epilogue

SISKO STOOD IN front of the spacedock's immense observation window and eyed the vessel that loomed before him out in space. A Miranda-class ship, it displayed all the usual characteristics.

A short, barrel-like hull. An almost painfully compact aft-sensor array. And a pair of low-slung, squared-off plasma nacelles, which were themselves almost as big as the rest of the ship.

Not the most elegant vessel ever designed, the captain mused. But then, esthetics weren't the primary consideration when it came to ships that could span the galaxy.

It was the technology inside the thing that counted. And perhaps even more important, it was the crew that manned it.

Sisko turned to his right, taking in Zar and Thorn at

a glance. Like him, they were intent on the Miranda-class vessel, on its every corner and curve. Turning to his left, he saw Graal and Laffer were likewise engaged.

Starfleet had had a somewhat larger contingent in mind for this event. Unfortunately it hadn't worked out that way.

"She's a beauty," said Thorn.

"Just like her predecessor," Zar confirmed.

Chief O'Brien had expressed a similar opinion just a little while earlier, as they were entering Mars orbit in the *Defiant*. Dax, aware of the captain's reservations about the commissioning, had remained silent on the subject.

Sisko's eyes were drawn to the designation on the nacelles—the only detail that set the ship apart from the one on which he'd served. It read NCC-31911-A.

His Saratoga had been NCC-31911—no suffix. It had been the standard, the template—the *original*.

"Sorry I'm late," said a voice that echoed from the other side of the observation lounge.

The captain turned and saw Commander Vincenzo approaching them. The commander, a friendly man with dark eyes and a neat black beard, had served as supervisor on the *Saratoga-A* project.

What's more, he was slated for a promotion—to take command of the vessel whose construction he had overseen. But then, good officers never stayed at Utopia Planitia for very long. It was usually more of a stepping-stone to something else.

"We had a little problem with the dock's tractor beams," Vincenzo explained, "but everything's in working order again."

Sisko managed a smile. "That's all right. We're not in any hurry."

He shook the commander's hand, acknowledging the bond between them. After all, one had served aboard a *Saratoga* and the other was about to. If they had nothing more than that in common, it was still a lot.

Talk about your ironies, the captain thought. After the disaster at Wolf 359, he had spent nearly three years building ships at Utopia Planitia. Had he remained at the fleet yards instead of reluctantly taking the job at *Deep Space Nine,* the construction of the *Saratoga-A* could have been *his* project.

Taking up a position next to Thorn, Vincenzo cleared his throat and tapped his Starfleet communicator. "We're ready, Lieutenant. You may proceed."

Sisko was familiar with the procedure, having witnessed it so many times before. Somewhere on the spacedock, a small airlock was opening and a champagne bottle was being expelled.

"Can you see it yet?" breathed Laffer, tilting her head toward the Craynid.

Graal shook her head. "No, not yet."

But a moment later the bottle drifted into view, caught now in the grip of a finely tuned tractor beam. Its flight pattern dictated by the ebb and flow of directed gravitons, the champagne flew end over end toward its objective.

As Sisko observed its flight, he remembered Dax's words. "Don't do it for all those others—do it for yourself, Benjamin. Because you're alive. Because you gave everything you had to that proud old ship. And most of all, because deep down inside, you really *want* to."

Here was the test of that advice—a test that could be made only in the face of the experience itself. While the champagne bottle made its slow, graceful journey through space, the captain examined his feelings.

They were like alien life forms he had never met, with the potential to be either hostile or friendly—it was difficult to know which right off the bat. And like actual aliens, he approached them with patience and an open mind and a healthy helping of caution.

People and events flooded his mind. Captain Saros frowning at his chessboard . . . Laffer befuddling the Cardassians on Mariphasa 4 . . . Graal repairing a damaged plasma conduit . . . Thorn making short work of a drunken Nausicaan on a long-ago shore leave . . .

By the time the bottle completed its voyage and smashed into the saucer section, spraying champagne and glass fragments in every direction, Sisko had come to understand the aliens within him.

They were friendly, all right. Friendlier than he ever would have dreamed possible. He remembered so many good times on his *Saratoga,* so many courageous times, the ship's destruction seemed only a part of a larger tapestry.

A tapestry of hope. Of enlightenment. And ultimately, despite everything, of victory.

Dax had been right, he realized. He *was* glad to be here. In fact, he had never been gladder—or prouder—to be anywhere in his life. If Jennifer had been standing here beside him, she would have felt the same way—he was certain of it.

Out of the corner of his eye, he saw Vincenzo lean forward and smile at him past Zar and Thorn. "May she acquit herself half as well as *your Saratoga,* Captain."

Sisko turned to him. "*My Saratoga* is just a memory, Mr. Vincenzo." He smiled back. "Now it's your turn. Go make some memories of your own."

ACCEPTED AROUND THE COUNTRY, AROUND THE WORLD, AND AROUND THE GALAXY!

- No Annual Fee
- Low introductory APR for cash advances and balance transfers
- Free trial membership in The Official STAR TREK Fan Club upon card approval*
- Discounts on selected STAR TREK Merchandise

To apply for the STAR TREK MasterCard today, call

1-800-775-TREK

Transporter Code: SKYD